D0484322

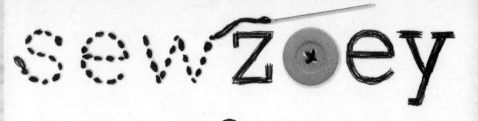

sew zoey

A CHANGE
OF LACE

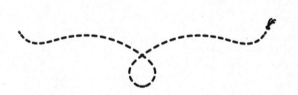

written by
Chloe Taylor

illustrated by
Nancy Zhang

Simon Spotlight
New York   London   Toronto   Sydney   New Delhi

SIMON SPOTLIGHT
An imprint of Simon & Schuster Children's Publishing Division
1230 Avenue of the Americas, New York, New York 10020
First Simon Spotlight hardcover edition October 2014
Copyright © 2014 by Simon & Schuster, Inc.
All rights reserved, including the right of reproduction in whole or in part in any form.
SIMON SPOTLIGHT and colophon are registered trademarks of Simon & Schuster, Inc.
Text by Sarah Darer Littman
Designed by Laura Roode
For information about special discounts for bulk purchases, please contact Simon & Schuster Special Sales at 1-866-506-1949 or business@simonandschuster.com.
Manufactured in the United States of America 0914 FFG
10 9 8 7 6 5 4 3 2 1
ISBN 978-1-4814-1962-8 (hc)
ISBN 978-1-4814-1961-1 (pbk)
ISBN 978-1-4814-1963-5 (eBook)
Library of Congress Catalog Card Number 2014942150

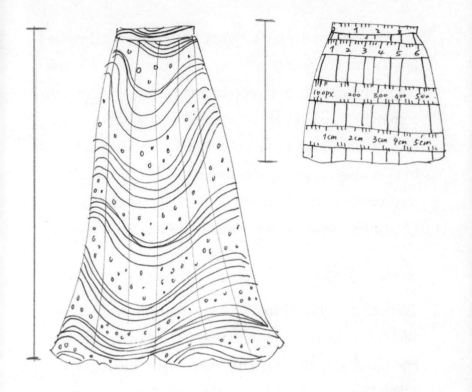

CHAPTER 1

The Long and the Short of It

Can you believe school starts next week?! Summer vacation always seems so long at the beginning, and then, at the end, it seems like it flashed by in an instant. All of a sudden it's about to be over, as if time magically starts to speed up in August.

It's been a really fun summer, getting to visit Daphne Shaw's studio, going to sleepaway camp for the first time, and taking a screen-printing class, but there's something exciting about starting a new school year, too. I'm designing a new outfit for the first day of school, but I'm keeping that under wraps for now. Instead, here are "the long and the short of it" skirts inspired by how I feel about time this summer. I hope you like them!

"What do you think, Marie Antoinette?" Zoey Webber asked her dressmaker's dummy as she put the final touches on the sketch for her back-to-school outfit. "Is this a winner or is it just . . . weird? I can't make up my mind."

The problem with Marie Antoinette was that being a headless dress form, she wasn't very forthcoming with her opinion.

Zoey sighed and looked at the pictures she'd printed out after watching a movie from the 1960s. They were of an Italian actress wearing a wide-legged halter-top jumpsuit. Zoey'd thought it was such a cool and different look, perfect for her to update with Zoey magic. But now, comparing the sixties outfit to her sketch, she wasn't so sure.

Just then the doorbell rang, interrupting her musings.

"Hey, Zo! The Holbrookes are here!" her brother, Marcus, announced from the bottom of the stairs.

Zoey slipped on her flip-flops, grabbed her purse and cell phone, and ran downstairs. She had a mall date with one of her best friends, Priti, to help her shop for a new back-to-school outfit.

"See you later, Marcus!" she called on the way out the door.

Zoey slid into the backseat next to Priti. "I can't believe school starts next week," she said. "I'm excited, but I'm still not sure if I'm ready."

"This summer has gone by so quickly," Mrs. Holbrooke said. "It seems like only yesterday you girls got out of school. A lot has happened since then, hasn't it?"

"You can say that again," Priti said with a sigh. She was still adjusting to the idea that her parents were getting a divorce and to the fact that her dad had moved out of the family home.

Mrs. Holbrooke gave Priti a worried look in the rearview mirror, which transformed into a cheerful smile the minute she caught Zoey's eye. "Well, you'll have to pick out a great outfit to wow everyone on the first day, right, Priti?"

"Uh-huh. Sure," Priti agreed without any of her normal bounce and enthusiasm.

Zoey wondered what was going on—had Priti and her mom had a fight before she had gotten into the car?

She spent the rest of the ride to the mall describing how she came up with the idea for her back-to-school outfit and asking Priti and Mrs. Holbrooke what they thought about the idea.

"I think it sounds fab," Priti said. "Why are you worrying so much, Zo? You were voted Best Dressed last year!"

"That just means I have more of a reputation to keep up!" Zoey said.

Mrs. Holbrooke pulled up outside the mall.

"I'm sure you'll look adorable, Zoey. You always do," she said. "I'll see you in a few hours. And you know the rules. . . . Don't talk to strangers, and call if you're even going to be a minute late for pick-up time."

As she drove off, Priti dragged Zoey toward the mall doors. "Come on! Let's shop till we drop!"

The girls browsed a few of the popular chain stores before ending up at their favorite clothing shop, My Best Friend's Closet. While Priti browsed, Zoey picked out a few outfits she knew her friend would love—colorful clothes, sparkly accessories, an adorable belt with a fake jeweled buckle.

She walked over to the display rack where Priti was standing.

"What do you think?" she said, holding up the clothes she'd picked out. "Perfect, right? Do you want to try them on?"

"Sure," Priti said, taking the clothes from her.

But Zoey noticed that before she walked to the dressing room to try them on, Priti grabbed a bunch of black clothes off a rack where she must have placed them while she'd been browsing.

That's odd, Zoey thought. Her friend was usually the queen of bright colors.

Priti came out wearing the first of the outfits Zoey'd picked for her.

"It looks awesome!" Zoey said.

Priti looked at her reflection in the mirror.

"I don't know. I'm not . . ." She paused, turning to look at it from another angle. "Let me try on the other one."

Zoey waited, wondering what Priti didn't like about the first outfit, which looked really good on her.

The second outfit looked even better on Priti than the first.

"What do you think?" Zoey asked.

"It's cute," Priti said. "I like it."

"Great!" Zoey said. "Just in time, because I'm getting hungry."

"I just want to try on one more thing," Priti said. "I'll meet you by the register."

When Priti went to the register to pay, all the clothes she was carrying were completely . . . black.

Zoey was surprised. Seeing a striped scarf hanging nearby, she took it from the display and draped it around Priti's neck.

"What do you think? It would brighten up your outfit a little."

Priti shrugged and removed the scarf from around her neck, placing it back on the display.

"It's nice, but I'm good without it."

"What about the jeweled belt?" Zoey suggested.

"No, it's okay. I'm just going to buy the jeans and the shirt."

As Priti paid for her purchases, Zoey wondered what was going on with her friend. Maybe Priti wanted to experiment with her style, and there definitely was nothing wrong with that. Zoey was all about being adventurous with clothes.

It was just . . . going from glitzy to goth seemed pretty *dramatic*. On the other hand, Zoey thought, Priti had always had a flair for the dramatic.

"I don't know about you, but I'm starving," Priti said, hooking her shopping bag over her shoulder. "Let's hit the food court."

After they got their food, the girls were looking for a table to eat at when Priti hissed, "Zo, is that *Shannon Chang* over by Lola's Lattes?" Shannon was friends with Ivy Wallace and Bree Sharpe, girls who often teased Zoey and her friends at school.

"*Oh my gosh*, yes it is," Zoey said. "Let's go the other way."

They found a table on the opposite side of the food court, next to a pillar, so they were out of sight.

Or so they thought. A few minutes later, Zoey caught sight of Shannon heading straight in their direction.

"She's coming over here," she told Priti in an undertone.

"Why?" Priti wondered.

"I don't know!" Zoey whispered.

They watched Shannon wind her way toward them, carrying a bag from a pricey designer shoe store.

"Hi, Zoey!" she said when she arrived at their table. "Hey, Priti."

"Hi, Shannon," Zoey said. "What's up?"

"Um . . . nothing much. Just . . . uh . . . doing a little shopping." She paused and stood there, looking awkward. "What are you guys up to?"

Priti looked pointedly at the trays of food on the table. "Eating lunch."

"Right," Shannon said, her cheeks flushing.

Zoey and Priti exchanged furtive glances as Shannon stood by the table in an uncomfortable silence. It was obvious she wanted something—but what?

"So . . . uh . . . Zoey . . . I was wondering if maybe you could maybe, you know . . . um, help me pick out a back-to-school outfit?"

Priti, who'd just taken a sip of soda, started coughing. Zoey figured Priti was as taken aback as she was that *Shannon Chang* was asking *her* for fashion advice.

"Um . . . okay," Zoey said.

Shannon smiled. "Great. We can go when you guys are finished eating."

Priti, who'd recovered from her coughing fit, gave Zoey a *What are you doing?* look.

"How about we meet at Urban Chic in, like, fifteen minutes?" Shannon suggested.

"Sounds like a plan," Zoey said. "See you in a few."

As soon as Shannon had walked out of earshot, Priti leaned across the table and asked, "*Are you crazy?* I bet this is just a setup for a prank. Ivy and Bree are probably somewhere in the mall, waiting to take a video when Shannon trips you or pushes you into the fountain or something."

Zoey wasn't 100 percent confident about Shannon's motives, but she didn't think she'd go *that* far.

"I don't know. I mean, we used to be friends. And Shannon's confessed in secret that she reads Sew Zoey, so she must be a little interested in fashion, right?"

"*Kate* reads Sew Zoey, and she doesn't care that much about fashion," Priti argued.

"But that's different," Zoey pointed out. "Kate's one of my best friends. Besides, you know, Shannon was in my screen-printing class this summer and she was really nice to me then. She even helped me make the T-shirts for Marcus's band." She finished the last of her smoothie. "I think Shannon's being genuine."

"I don't know," Priti said, clearly still skeptical. "Just be careful, okay?"

Shopping with her former best friend and one of her current BFFs was seriously awkward, Zoey decided. Shannon acted as if Priti wasn't there, while Priti kept giving Zoey *See, I told you* looks.

"How about this?" Zoey said, holding up a cute denim skirt.

"I don't know . . . ," Shannon said. "I don't think it's me."

Priti sighed, loudly, and checked the clock on her cell for the third time in ten minutes.

Shannon finally acknowledged Priti's existence by giving her a dirty look.

Zoey was beginning to wish she were at home working on her own outfit instead of helping everyone else with theirs.

She found a pair of capris in a vivid cobalt blue and showed them to Shannon.

"These are adorable, don't you think?"

Shannon shrugged. "They are, but . . . I'm not sure."

Zoey definitely wished she were back at her worktable. She wasn't having a good time. Not at all.

Priti checked her cell again.

"Uh-oh! Look at the time—can't keep Mom waiting!"

"Sorry, Shannon," Zoey said. "I guess we just didn't have any luck today."

"It's okay," Shannon said. "Um . . . maybe we could come back tomorrow and look again?"

Priti was behind Shannon, shaking her head so vigorously that Zoey was afraid Priti was going to hurt her neck. But there must have been something of the old Shannon in the request, because Zoey found herself saying "Sure, it'll be fun" and arranging to meet Shannon at two the next day at My Best Friend's Closet.

"What possessed you to say yes?" Priti asked as they walked out to meet her mom. "I don't understand."

"I don't know," Zoey said. "Because she used to be my best friend, and she asked me?"

"I don't trust her, Zo," Priti said. "Not the teensiest tiniest bit."

On the ride home, Priti went even further.

"You should call Shannon and cancel your plans for tomorrow," she urged Zoey.

"I can't do that!" Zoey exclaimed. "I already told her I would."

"Tell her you have a doctor's appointment you forgot about," Priti said. "Make something up."

"I don't want to lie to her," Zoey said. "I'd feel bad."

"You shouldn't be encouraging your friends to lie, Priti," Mrs. Holbrooke admonished.

"It's not that, Mom. It's just that Shannon's been mean to Zoey at school, and I don't want her to get hurt again."

"Wanting to protect your friend is a good intention. Telling her to lie . . . not so much," Priti's mom said.

Priti sighed. "Well, however you do it, you've got to figure out a way to get out of going shopping with Shannon tomorrow, Zoey," she said. "I'm telling you, she's up to no good. Trust me."

When Zoey got home, she wasn't sure what to do. Deep down, she shared some of Priti's concerns about Shannon's sincerity and wondered why her old friend suddenly wanted her advice after being distant for so long. But they'd had a good time in their class together during the summer. Maybe there was a chance they could patch things up, even if they weren't BFFs anymore.

After getting a snack, Zoey picked up the phone and called Kate. She explained her dilemma and asked what to do.

"I agree with Priti," Kate said. "I'm worried you could be walking into a trap."

Zoey thanked her for her opinion, but inside, it just made her feel discouraged. Next she called Libby. Zoey was surprised that Libby seemed to agree with Priti and Kate.

"Do you really think she wants your fashion advice, Zo?" Libby asked. "Think about all the times she's stood there and smiled while Ivy's made fun of your outfits."

"Well, you and Priti and Kate all seem to feel the same way, so you're probably right, but she was really nice to me over the summer, you know?"

"Trust your gut, Zoey," Libby replied. "But I don't want you to get hurt."

When they said good-bye, Zoey had a sick feeling in the pit of her stomach. It was true. Shannon hadn't been much of a friend over the last year.

Shannon had watched and even joined in when Ivy and Bree were being unkind to Zoey.

"Everything okay, honey?" her father asked at dinner. Zoey was uncharacteristically quiet.

"No," Zoey admitted. "I just don't know what to do." She explained her Shannon dilemma. "Part of me thinks everyone's right, and maybe I should cancel, but another part of me thinks that maybe she has changed, and what if I'm not being fair?"

"Well, you know what we say in sports—no pain, no gain," her father said.

Zoey nodded.

"It's like that with relationships, too. There's always a risk of getting hurt, but if you don't give people the benefit of the doubt, then you might miss out on the good stuff, too," Mr. Webber explained.

"So you think I should go?" Zoey said.

"You had a nice time with her this summer, right? What's the harm of giving her another chance for an hour or two?"

Being pranked by Ivy? Being laughed at?

Zoey thought about what her father said, and realized that maybe she should just be brave and give Shannon the benefit of the doubt.

"I will," Zoey said. "Even if my best friends think I'm crazy."

---------- CHAPTER 2 ----------

Color Me Confused

Things really are changing this year—and school hasn't even started yet! Have you ever had a friend, who has always loved certain things, suddenly change and have completely different tastes? It's not a bad change, necessarily, but it's sudden. And other people are acting totally different too, and I don't know what to think. This all sounds vague and mysterious, doesn't it? But it's hard to say exactly what I mean without using names.

The one thing I can say is that I'm confused—really, seriously confused by it all.

It makes me wonder what other changes the new school year is going to bring. When I think about it, last year at this time I had just barely started Sew Zoey—and look at all the amazing things that have happened since then because of it!

Today I'm attaching a sketch I did just for fun. It's nice to zone out and not worry about all this stuff and just draw.

When Zoey arrived at My Best Friend's Closet the next day, Shannon greeted her with such a big smile, Zoey was glad she hadn't listened to her friends and canceled.

"Thanks for doing this, Zoey," she said. "I've been really freaking out about the whole back-to-school thing."

"It's nothing to worry about," Zoey assured her. "You should try to have fun with it."

"That's easier said than done when you're friends with Ivy Wallace." Shannon sighed. "She's insisting that Bree and I get both a specific style of designer shoes and the same kind of messenger bag that she likes for back to school, which wouldn't be so bad except they're both really expensive."

"Can't you explain to her that you can't afford both?" Zoey asked.

Shannon laughed. "Explain not being able to afford stuff *to Ivy*? No way. She says that anyone who doesn't have both the shoes and the messenger bag isn't cool—and the last thing I want to do is get on Ivy's bad side."

Zoey could understand that. She'd always been on Ivy's bad side, for reasons she didn't know, and it wasn't a whole lot of fun. But there was one thing she couldn't understand.

"Why are you friends with her if she'd give you a hard time just because you can't afford something?"

"Ivy's not that bad, once you get to know her,"

Shannon insisted. "She's a lot of fun to be around."

I guess . . . if you aren't the one she's making fun of, Zoey thought.

"It's just that I'm getting a little sick of being told what to wear," Shannon continued. "And besides, my parents gave me a budget for back-to-school shopping. It was enough to buy the shoes, which were pretty expensive. I bought them yesterday, because I really liked them, but now it doesn't leave me very much to buy a whole lot else. It's *definitely* not enough for the messenger bag."

"Could you ask for the messenger bag as an early Christmas present or something?" Zoey suggested as she browsed a rack of shirts.

"I tried that already. My parents said that the money they've given me is as much as their budget allows, and if I want any extra, I have to babysit," Shannon complained. "But there's no way I can babysit enough before school starts to earn the money to buy something that expensive."

She held up a chartreuse shirt.

Zoey shook her head. "Maybe in a different color?" she asked.

Shannon shrugged and put it back on the rack.

"My parents say they can't understand why it's so important to me to fit in. And they keep asking what kind of friend would demand that I buy things that are so expensive."

"I wonder that too, to tell you the truth," Zoey said.

Shannon gave Zoey a sharp look, as if trying to determine whose side she was on.

"Whatever. I like clothes, and I love reading your blog. Can you help me to find my own style, but not so much that Ivy will reject me? I mean, I don't want to totally stand out, the way you do."

"Okaaay . . . ," Zoey said, not sure if Shannon meant that last part as a compliment or . . . not.

"Ever since we stopped wearing uniforms, I've just been wearing whatever Ivy tells me to. Now that I want to be a little different, I have no idea what to buy," Shannon said, holding up a T-shirt that read LIKE A BOSS. "What do you think?"

Zoey shook her head. "You can do better."

"I bought the shoes. Here," Shannon said, showing Zoey a picture of them on her cell phone. "If you help me find a few cute cheap things to make up the rest of the outfit, I can keep Ivy happy but still be myself, too."

"Let's see what we can find, then," Zoey said. "Ooh! What about these?"

She showed Shannon a pair of pink leopard-print jeans.

"Those are *adorable!*" Shannon exclaimed. "Let me go try them on!"

Zoey made her wait till they'd picked out a few more items, but in the end the leopard-print jeans were still the winner.

"They match my shoes perfectly," Shannon said.

"And they make a statement," Zoey said.

"But without standing out too much, right?" Shannon asked.

"No, not too much," Zoey assured her. "Leopard print is in."

"What should I wear with them?"

"You probably have a basic tee at home, right? That would go without competing with the pattern on the pants," Zoey suggested.

"I guess," Shannon said. "Can you maybe come

over to help me pick out something?"

While they'd been hanging out, Zoey had caught glimpses of the old Shannon, the one who had had sleepovers with her in elementary school and played with Draper when he was a puppy, who hadn't cared what Bree and Ivy thought. It made her realize how much she missed that Shannon.

"Okay," she said.

Her dad had been right. It *was* worth giving Shannon another chance.

"Zoey . . . I've got another favor to ask," Shannon said after she'd paid for the jeans.

"What's that?"

"Do you mind keeping the fact that you helped me with my back-to-school outfit a secret?" Shannon asked. "It's just that . . . if Ivy finds out you chose these pants, she'll probably pick on you even more, out of spite."

Wow. *Maybe my BFFs were right after all.*

It hurt Zoey's feelings that Shannon wanted her to be a secret stylist instead of being open about it. Was she really trying to protect her from Ivy, or was Shannon ashamed of hanging out with her? But on the other hand, Shannon did seem genuinely appreciative of her help, and they'd had a good time together. Was it worth the trade-off?

"Okay," she agreed reluctantly. But as she went to meet Marcus for her ride home from the mall, she wondered if she'd made the right decision.

Sewing always helped Zoey feel better, so she went straight up to her worktable to put the finishing touches on her back-to-school outfit. The wide-legged jumper looked so great on Sophia Loren, and Zoey loved the way the excess material almost made it look like she was wearing a skirt. It was really different from anything she'd ever made or worn before. But different was good. After winning Best Dressed in the yearbook last year, she was feeling more confident about herself and wanted to start off this year with a memorable outfit.

When she finished the final stitches, Zoey decided to try it on and model it for Dad and Marcus. She admired herself in the mirror and then went downstairs, loving the swishy feel of the wide-legged pants as she walked.

"*Ta-da!* What do you think of my back-to-school outfit?" she asked, striking a pose in the kitchen, where Dad and Marcus were preparing dinner. Aunt Lulu and her boyfriend, John, were coming over.

Her dramatic entrance was met by dead silence, except for the announcer on the radio giving the results of the previous night's sports contests. And then Dad turned off the radio, and it was totally quiet. None of the usual exclamations of "It's great, Zoey!" that she'd grown to expect.

"Honey . . . if you love it, I love it," Dad said.

"Honestly, Zoey, I just think this one is . . . off the mark," Marcus jumped in.

"Off the mark how?" Zoey asked. "It's different, I know, but I think it's in a good way."

She saw her father exchange glances with her brother.

"Zo, I'll always support you being different, you know that," Dad said.

"True. But I don't want you to look ridiculous," Marcus added.

"*You think it's ridiculous?!*" Zoey wailed.

"It's just a little over the top, Zoey," continued

Marcus. "I don't want you to go from Best Dressed to Best Mess."

"You know I think you've got a great talent, and I usually love all your ideas . . . ," Dad said.

"You hate it too?" Zoey said. She wasn't used to her dad not liking her designs. He was usually so supportive.

"'Hate' is a strong word," Dad said. "I'm just wondering if your brother is right. But what do I know?"

Zoey stood facing her critics with her hands on her hips, her chin held high.

"Well, I'm going to wait till Aunt Lulu comes and get *her* opinion," she said.

"Good idea," Dad said. "I'll be the first to admit that I'm a fashion fossil."

"We'll see," Zoey said with a sniff.

When Zoey answered the door to let in Aunt Lulu and John, her aunt's dog, Buttons, scampered in and greeted Zoey enthusiastically.

Zoey picked up Buttons and cuddled her, carrying her into the kitchen.

"See, Dad, Buttons likes my outfit!"

"What's this? Is there an outfit controversy?" Aunt Lulu asked.

Zoey put down Buttons so she could twirl for her aunt and John, giving them a full view of her swishy pant legs.

"I made this outfit for the first day of school, and Dad and Marcus think it's over the top and ridiculous," Zoey said. "But they aren't *fashionistas* like you and me. What do *you* think?"

Aunt Lulu and John studied the outfit.

"Well, I think it's cool," John said. "I can picture a sixties style icon, like Twiggy or Edie Sedgewick, wearing it."

Zoey was just beginning to get to know John, but her opinion of him immediately went up 200 percent.

"You totally got it!" she exclaimed. "It was inspired by a sixties movie I watched."

John smiled, and Zoey liked the way his smile twinkled in his eyes, too.

Aunt Lulu, however, was frowning.

"I don't know, Zo. I'm not sure if I love it or I hate it," she said. "I mean, I love the *idea*. I'm just not sure if I like it in reality. It feels a little too sophisticated for someone your age."

Zoey got a sinking feeling in her stomach by Aunt Lulu's words. She could discount her father's opinion, and even Marcus's, because neither of them were really experts in fashion, but Aunt Lulu was another story—she knew her stuff. She was an interior designer with a great sense of style.

"I think it'll be better when you're taller and have broader shoulders to balance out the wide legs," Aunt Lulu continued. "But the color and fabric is beautiful on you!"

"I guess I'll have to think about it some more," Zoey said. "I'll go change before dinner."

She went back up to her room to change into her shorts and T-shirt, but before she did, she took another look at herself in the full-length mirror. She *liked* the way she looked in the outfit.

Zoey figured she'd go with her gut. She thought it was cool and different in an *everything-old-is-new-again* kind of way, and besides, it made her feel good to wear it. That was what a good outfit should do, right?

She decided to call Kate to vent about her frustrations. But Kate had problems of her own.

"I'm so *bored*," she complained. "Resting my arm is no fun at all."

Kate was superathletic and was always going from one practice to another, but she'd strained her elbow recently, and the doctor had told her to rest her arm in a sling, so it could heal properly.

"I bet," Zoey said. "I'd go crazy if I couldn't use my arm. I wouldn't be able to sew anything!"

"Do you want to hang out tomorrow?" Kate asked.

Zoey was torn. She wanted to hang out with Kate, but she'd already promised Shannon that she'd go over to her house to help her with the rest of her outfit.

"I . . . can't. I've got plans with Shannon."

"*Shannon Chang? Really?*"

"Um . . . yeah."

"Oh . . . ," Kate said. "How about if I come too? It's the last day of vacation, and if I have to spend it sitting around the house again, I'm going to tear out my hair!"

Zoey hesitated. It was true Kate and Shannon had kind of been friends in elementary school, but it wasn't really because they had anything it common. It was more because they were both friends with Zoey. Shannon was Zoey's girly friend—they'd do each other's hair and play with dolls, which didn't interest sports-obsessed Kate at all.

Zoey didn't want to upset Kate, but she couldn't explain to her that she wouldn't be interested in what they were doing, because she couldn't explain why she was going over to Shannon's. Shannon had made her promise to keep it a secret, and she didn't want to break her promise and risk losing the headway she'd made rebuilding their friendship.

"It would . . . just be awkward," she said. "I'll call you later, okay?"

"Okay," Kate said.

Zoey felt bad when she hung up. She could tell Kate was upset. How could she be a good friend to everyone without making anyone upset?

CHAPTER 3

Old Is New Again

I love buying—and making—new clothes, but isn't it great when you slip on a really old denim jacket that's been washed a lot of times, so it's soft and already broken in? Marcus was going to get rid of this jacket, because it's too small for him now, but

I salvaged it and gave it a new life by adding sequins and embroidering peace signs and flowers. I love putting it on because it's new to me, but it feels as comfortable as getting together with an old friend. You know, even when you haven't hung out in a long time, but then you do and you have fun, and you wonder why you ever stopped? It's fun to make old clothes new again. Do you think it's possible to do it with friendships, too?

Walking into the Changs' house was just like putting on Marcus's old worn-in denim jacket, Zoey thought. Even though she hadn't been there in ages, she felt totally comfortable, and it was nice to get to see Shannon's family again. Shannon's parents told her how much they missed seeing her.

Daisy, Shannon's seven year-old sister, danced around the kitchen, singing "Zoey's here! Zoey's here!"

Zoey smiled, happy to see Daisy. "You've grown so much!"

But Shannon told Daisy to leave Zoey alone and

.to stop being so annoying. Brandon, Shannon's nine year-old brother, asked if Zoey wanted to play Mario Kart with him.

Before Zoey could answer, Shannon said, "She can't. We're going upstairs."

"Can I come?" Daisy asked.

"Not now, Daisy," Shannon said. "Zoey and I have stuff to do."

Zoey mouthed *Sorry* to the crestfallen Daisy as she followed Shannon out of the kitchen and up to her bedroom.

Despite her limited budget, Shannon had a lot of choices in her closet and drawers. Zoey picked out some options, and Shannon tried them on with the pink leopard-print pants and her designer shoes to see which looked best. When she finally decided, they both sat cross-legged on Shannon's bed.

"So what are *you* wearing on the first day?" Shannon asked. "Have you decided yet?"

"It's a surprise," Zoey said. "I think I know, but I haven't one hundred percent decided."

"Is it a *Sew Zoey* creation?" Shannon asked.

Zoey nodded.

"Oh, show me, *please!*" Shannon begged. "Can't I at least see a sketch?"

Zoey wondered if showing Shannon was a good idea. But she'd been having such a good time with her that she relented.

"Okay," Zoey said, digging into her bag for her sketchbook. She flipped to the page with the wide-legged jumper outfit.

"That's amazing!" Shannon exclaimed. "You're so creative!"

"You really think so?" Zoey asked. "You're not just saying that?"

"No, I'm not just saying it. I really do think it's awesome. I wish I could design and make my own clothes like you do," Shannon said.

"Thanks," Zoey said, smiling. It meant a lot to Zoey that her old friend liked the outfit and thought what she did was cool. And it made her even more determined to wear her creation to school the next day.

When she got home from Shannon's, Allie, Marcus's girlfriend, was over.

"Allie, you have to convince Zoey not to wear the crazy outfit she designed to school tomorrow," Marcus said.

"Marcus!" Zoey exclaimed. "It's none of your business what I wear!"

"It's because I care, Zo," Marcus said. "I'm doing this because I love you."

"I'm not sure I want to get in the middle of this," Allie said. "But if you want a second opinion, I'll take a look."

"It wouldn't be a second opinion," grumbled Zoey. "It'll be, like, a seventh or eighth opinion."

"Well, okay, if you want *another* opinion," Allie said. "Just offering . . ."

Allie *did* have really good fashion sense. Maybe it was worth getting her opinion, just in case.

"I'll go put it on," Zoey said, heading upstairs to her room to get changed into her outfit.

She walked back downstairs, feeling confident that Allie was going to love it the same way Shannon did. But the expression on Allie's face told her she didn't.

"I hate to say it, Zoey, but I think Marcus

is right about this one," Allie said. "It's too . . . costume-y. I just think it's a little much for the first day of school. Maybe you could alter it—slim down the legs, so they aren't quite as wide?"

"I don't have time to do alterations that big," Zoey said.

She wasn't sure she wanted to even if she *did* have time.

"Well, if I were you, I'd find another outfit to wear," Allie suggested. "You've designed and made so many cute things this summer. I just don't think you need to be quite so . . . *extreme* on the first day."

"Thanks, anyway, for the advice," Zoey said, even though she didn't like what Allie had suggested at all.

As she walked back up to her room, Zoey debated what to do. Allie *wasn't* her. She was the one and only Zoey Webber, and she'd gotten used to being someone who stood out and took risks with her style. She wanted to wear what she wanted to wear, and didn't she win Best Dressed last year after doing just that? She was done getting everyone else's opinions. She was going to wear her outfit, and that was that!

Kate and Zoey sat on the bus together as always, and Zoey was relieved that her friend didn't seem to be upset about not having gotten together the day before. Kate was wearing one of the cute sling covers Zoey had made for her.

"I can't believe how glad I am that school's starting," Kate said. "Without being able to do sports, it seems like every day is a week long."

"You're usually so busy with practices, we hardly see you," Zoey said.

"I know. I mean, I'm excited to be able to spend more time with you guys, but I miss going to practice." Kate sighed. "I like the routine, and I always feel better afterward, even if I didn't want to go."

"Hopefully, the doctor will let you go back soon," Zoey said.

She'd hate to not be able to sketch or sew for a whole month. No wonder Kate was feeling so antsy.

When they got to school, Ms. Austen, the

principal, was waiting out front to greet all the students, as was her custom.

"Look at Ms. Austen's new haircut! It's so cute!" Kate exclaimed.

"It makes her look younger, don't you think?" Zoey said.

Kate agreed.

"Welcome back!" Ms. Austen said, greeting the two girls. She looked Zoey's outfit up and down. "Interesting design, Zoey."

Zoey got the impression that Ms. Austen was in the Dad and Marcus camp when it came to her back-to-school outfit. But before she could worry too much about it, Ms. Austen said, "Girls, I'd like you to meet our new student, Josephine. She's from Paris, and she will be living with her aunt and uncle in the United States for a while to help her learn English. Josie, meet Kate and Zoey."

"I'm very 'appy to meet you," Josie said with a strong French accent.

Zoey liked her right away. She had a friendly smile . . . and a really cool alphabet-print scarf looped around her neck.

"Great to meet you, too!" Zoey said. "Let us know if you need help or want someone to sit with at lunch."

"*Merci*—I mean, thank you," Josie said.

"Definitely," Kate said. "We'll introduce you to our other friends too."

"I knew I could count on you to be a good welcoming committee," Ms. Austen said.

"Thanks," Zoey said. "By the way, I love your haircut."

"Why, thank you," Ms. Austen said. "I wasn't sure at first, but now I'm feeling more confident with it."

Unlike how I'm feeling about my outfit, Zoey thought.

"Oh, look, there's Libby's bus," Kate said.

They walked over to greet Libby as she got off the bus. Shannon was standing nearby with Ivy and Bree. She was wearing the outfit Zoey had picked out for her.

"I *love* those leopard-print pants," Zoey overheard Ivy telling Shannon. "I'm going to have to get a pair myself."

"Me too," Bree chimed in.

So much for Shannon having her own look, Zoey thought.

Then Ivy looked over in Zoey's direction and snickered. "Looks like the circus came to town and forgot to take the clown with them when they left."

Bree laughed. Shannon didn't laugh. When Zoey looked at her, Shannon gave Zoey an apologetic glance, but she didn't say anything. Zoey was torn. It would give her so much satisfaction to be able to tell Ivy that *she* was the one who'd picked out the leopard-print jeans that Ivy liked so much. She wanted to say it more than anything. But she'd promised Shannon she'd keep it a secret, and a promise was a promise.

That just made it all the more hurtful when Shannon didn't say anything to stick up for her, especially since she'd said in private how much she liked Zoey's outfit.

Zoey bit her lip and walked away.

"Why do you hang out with Shannon when she just stands there when Ivy's being so mean to you?" Kate asked.

"Seriously," Libby agreed. "I don't get it."

Zoey wasn't sure she understood it either. But she was saved from having to answer because just then, Priti arrived, dressed from top to toe in black, with black nail polish and streaks of blue hair.

Priti's appearance didn't come as quite as much of a shock to Zoey as it was to Kate and Libby. She'd at least had some inkling of Priti's dramatic change in style from their shopping expedition at the mall. The blue hair streaks were a surprise, though. She wondered how Mr. and Mrs. Holbrooke reacted to *that*.

Kate and Libby couldn't believe their eyes.

"Who are you and what have you done with Priti?" Kate asked.

"Is that a costume?" Libby asked.

"No, it's not a costume," Priti said. "It's my new look."

"B-but . . . it's so . . . ," Kate stammered.

"So what?" Priti asked.

"*Different*," Libby said. "I mean, from how you normally dress."

"What did your mom say when she saw your hair?" Zoey asked.

Priti was about to answer when a brown-haired boy in khakis and a polo shirt said, "Hi, Priti."

Priti stared at him blankly.

Zoey didn't recognize him either. She wondered if he was a new student. But if he was, how did he know Priti?

"It's me, Miles," the mystery boy revealed. "Your sister Sashi and my sister Nicole were in orchestra together this summer. Remember?"

Zoey couldn't believe it. She remembered Miles from last year. He was known as the Goth Kid because he had black hair and black nail polish and stud earrings, and he always wore black. In fact, he was always dressed in clothes just like Priti was wearing now!

"But, Miles . . . you look so . . . different!" Priti managed to say.

"So do you," Miles said. "It's almost like we . . . switched. Well, see you later, I guess."

"I can't believe it!" Priti exclaimed when he walked away. "We started hanging out when we had to wait for our sisters at orchestra rehearsal pickup. He was the one who inspired me to dress this way. I thought his look was so cool. So . . . what's made him go all *preppy*?"

"He looked just as surprised to see you dressed the way he *used* to look," Zoey observed.

"I didn't even recognize him," Libby said.

"Wait, Priti—you never answered my question about your hair," Zoey said. "What did your mom say about you dyeing it? Did she totally freak out?"

"She doesn't know," Priti said. "Because I didn't dye it. These are clip-ins."

Zoey couldn't help feeling relieved that the blue streaks weren't permanent.

"We haven't walked into the building yet and so much has already changed this year," Kate said. "I wonder what *else* is going to happen."

In the hallway between classes, Zoey bumped into her friend Gabe. Over the summer, she had run into him a few times but hadn't seen him since her brother's band's concert.

"Hi, Zoey," he said. "Did you have a good rest of the summer?"

"Yes," she said. "What about you?"

"Good," Gabe said. "How's the Sew Zoey Etsy site going?"

"Okay, I guess," Zoey said. "I mean, the sales aren't fantastic, but . . ."

"Don't forget, I can help you with the photographs," Gabe reminded her. "I learned a lot about lighting in the class I took this summer. There are all kinds of tricks I can use to make your designs really pop."

"Really? You'd do that?" Zoey said.

"Of course! It'll be cool," Gabe said. "How about Wednesday after school?"

"Sounds good," Zoey said.

She noticed that as she was talking, Gabe was looking over her shoulder, seemingly very interested in whatever he was seeing behind her. She turned and saw Josie, the French girl, coming down the hall toward them.

"Oh, hi, Josie," Zoey said. "How's your day going so far?"

"Comme ci, comme ça. A little confusing."

"Um . . . this is my friend Gabe Monaco," Zoey

said. "Josie's a new student from Paris."

"*Enchanté*, Josie," Gabe said. "*Ça va?*"

"*Oui, ça va bien. Tu parles français?*" Josie responded.

"*Un petit peu,*" Gabe said.

Zoey couldn't understand what they were saying, and she felt left out of the conversation. She couldn't help noticing how animated Gabe was when he talked to Josie too.

"I've got to get to class," Zoey said. "I'll see you later."

Gabe said, "Later, Zo," and Josie said, "*À bientôt,*" but neither seemed too aware that she was leaving. Zoey couldn't help feeling a little upset. Gabe had always been so attentive to her. But suddenly he seemed to have forgotten she existed. Her first day was turning out to be kind of a bust. Maybe she should have listened to the naysayers about her outfit after all. At least then she'd have felt better about one thing on her first day back at school.

She was glad to get together with her friends at lunch to see how everyone's day was going and to catch up.

"I can't wait till today is over," she said. "I'm kind of wishing I hadn't worn this."

"Don't let Ivy get you down, Zoey," Libby said. "Remember, you were the one voted Best Dressed last year, not her."

"I know," Zoey said. "But what if I've lost my touch?"

"Nobody gets it right all the time," Priti said. "You're entitled to a fashion faux pas once in a while."

"So you agree with Dad and Marcus and Allie? You think it *is* a faux pas?" Zoey asked.

Priti hesitated. "Well . . . if you want me to be totally honest . . . it's not my favorite outfit ever. I just don't think it flatters you the way your designs normally do."

"You look a little lost in the wide legs," Libby said. "Like you're a kid wearing grown-up pants or something."

It was the first time her friends had ever criticized her work so bluntly. It wasn't a great feeling.

"Don't be mad, Zoey," Kate said. "You know we love your stuff ninety-nine point nine percent of the time. If I had that kind of winning percentage in sports, I'd be doing a happy dance!"

"I guess," Zoey said.

"So guess what Mom's making me do after school." Kate sighed, obviously attempting to change the subject.

"What?" Priti asked.

"She's so sick of me hanging around the house, telling her I'm bored because I can't do sports, that she said I have to take *piano lessons*," Kate said.

"But what about your arm?" Zoey asked.

"The doctor said the finger movements wouldn't be too taxing, so it would be okay," Kate explained. "And Mom always wanted to be a professional concert pianist, so she's really been pushing the idea."

"That's awesome!" Libby exclaimed. "You'll love playing the piano. I've been taking lessons since I was little. We can play a duet together!"

"Well, give me a chance to learn how to play more than 'Chopsticks' first!" Kate laughed. "I guess I'm looking forward to it. It'll be fun to do something different for a change."

All Zoey could think about was going home and *changing* into something different. But she still had the whole afternoon—and more encounters with Ivy—to go.

Every time Zoey saw Ivy for the rest of the day, there was another snide remark about her outfit. It was bad enough when Ivy was by herself or just with Bree, but the times that hurt Zoey the most were when Shannon was there too and said nothing.

Why doesn't she say anything? Zoey thought as she walked to catch the bus after school.

"Is everything okay, Zoey?" Ms. Austen asked as Zoey walked by. "You look like you've had a tough first day."

Zoey sighed, and her eyes felt heavy with unshed tears.

"I think maybe Dad and Marcus were right. Maybe I shouldn't have worn this outfit to school," she said. "Maybe it is over the top and . . . well, ridiculous. I've gone from Best Dressed to Worst Dressed."

"I wouldn't go that far," Ms. Austen said, her

voice kind and gentle. "I'm really proud of you for always being willing to take risks and be true to yourself. Most middle-school kids just want to dress like everyone else—but no one can ever say that about Zoey Webber!"

"Usually, I really like being true to myself, but it's not so much fun when you make mistakes. Maybe that's why it's easier to dress like everyone else," Zoey said.

"Zoey, you have a special gift for fashion. I think you know that deep down. But you're human, and that means you're allowed to make mistakes once in a while."

Tell that to Ivy, Zoey thought.

"Give yourself a break, okay?" Ms. Austen said. "Tomorrow's another day for fashion."

Feeling a little bit better, Zoey headed for the bus. Ms. Austen was right. Tomorrow was another day, and she had plenty of ideas for new outfits!

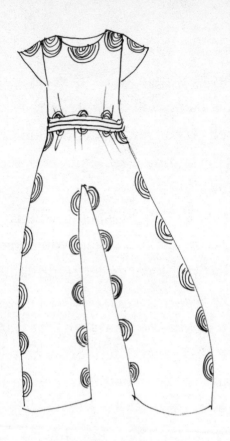

CHAPTER 4

Back in Time

Do you ever wish you could go back in time and have a do-over? I'm feeling like that about my back-to-school outfit. It was inspired by a sixties movie, and I thought it was really cool and retro, except updated with my own modern touches.

I still think its cool, but . . . well, let's just say that the reviews from everyone else were mixed! Dad and Marcus thought I was making a big mistake. They aren't the world's most fashionable guys, but they really care about me. Allie does have good fashion sense, and she wasn't crazy about it either. Aunt Lulu was on the fence. When I got dressed for school this morning, I almost wore something else. But then I thought: Shouldn't I stay true to my creative vision, even if people around me are telling me it's wrong?

So I did—and the reward was that I got to listen to this mean girl making fun of me all day. What's worse is that a certain person just stood there and didn't say anything, even though she'd told me she liked the design the day before.

Now I'm wondering—was I right to wear it or was I wrong? How do you know when to go with your gut and stay true to your ideas and when to listen to the critics and make changes?

The next day things went more smoothly for Zoey on the fashion front. But when she met her friends at lunch, she learned that things weren't as smooth for Kate and her new extracurricular activity.

"Learning to play the piano is *way* harder than I thought it would be," Kate complained. "Mom always makes it look so easy and fun when *she* plays. But now I have to learn how to do hard stuff, like reading music and practicing boring scales."

"Learning to read music isn't that hard," Libby assured her. "It just takes some getting used to."

"I hope you're right." Kate sighed. "Right now it's like trying to read gibberish. It's more fun when I get to mess around and play 'Chopsticks.'"

"Maybe think of playing scales like doing drills at soccer practice," Libby said. "They help your fingers the same way drills help your footwork."

"Soccer drills are more fun, though," Kate said. "At least I'm running around instead of sitting on a bench."

Zoey secretly wondered if Kate was going to last at piano lessons. But if she could give them half the determination she showed toward sports, she'd be fine.

"Speaking of running around," Libby said, "my

little sister, Sophie, was running around telling the entire first grade that the famous Sew Zoey made her dress *just for her.*"

"That's so adorable!" Zoey exclaimed.

"Mom said Sophie told her she felt like the queen of first grade," Libby said. "She said to tell you thank you!"

"I enjoyed making it for her," Zoey said. "Especially once I figured out I wasn't going crazy and losing everything and that it was Sophie who was taking the bits and pieces for her dollhouse!"

"I wish I felt like the queen of something fun," Priti grumbled. "Right now, I'm just the queen of shuttling back and forth between Mom's house and Dad's house. I wish I could turn back time, so that I was at camp and I still thought there was a chance my parents would stay together."

"It must be so hard," Zoey said, giving her friend's hand a sympathetic squeeze. She'd seen how Priti had reacted when she, Aunt Lulu, and Mr. Holbrooke had worked in secret to create a dream room for Priti at her dad's house. Even though she loved the room, Priti ended up crying because her father decorating a room for her made her realize her parents definitely weren't getting back together.

Priti adjusted the black rubber bracelets on her wrist, then picked up her bag and her tray.

"I've got to hit the restroom before class. See you later!" she said.

Her friends all watched her black-clad figure walk away through the crowded cafeteria.

"Do you think Priti's going to wear all black, all the time now?" Libby asked.

"I don't know," Zoey said. "When we went to the mall, I picked out all these typical Priti outfits, but she just wanted to buy the black pieces she'd chosen. So I suggested a scarf to brighten things up, but she still wasn't interested."

"I'm worried about her," Libby said. "It's so un-Priti to be dark and uncolorful. She's usually the queen of color and glitz!"

"Maybe she's just not feeling that colorful and glitzy with her parents getting divorced and her life being so topsy-turvy," Kate said. "I mean, what I'm going through isn't nearly as bad, but I don't feel like myself when I can't do sports."

"It's just so dramatic," Zoey pointed out. "One minute she's Miss More Color the Better, and the next minute she's Miss No Color at All."

"But Priti's always been dramatic," Kate argued. "She never does things halfway."

"That's true," Libby said. "But I hope this isn't permanent. I miss the old, colorful Priti."

"We'll just have to wait and see," Zoey said.

When Zoey got home from school, she checked Sew Zoey and was happy to see there were lots of helpful comments.

CrossStitchGal wrote:

You should definitely stay true to your vision, but it helps to find a core group of people you trust that you can ask for constructive criticism of your ideas. Then listen to their feedback without taking it personally—which can be hard sometimes!

Zigzagger wrote that she had a sewing circle called the Rippin' Stitchers:

We critique each others work. Sometimes the critiques can get a little "pointed" LOL! But we've learned to trust each other's judgment and be honest but kind!

There was even a comment from Zoey's fashion fairy godmother, DaphneShawNY:

Personally, I loved the design, but you're going to have to recognize that not everything you create will be a hit with everyone. When you're in this business—or indeed, any creative field—you have to learn to develop a thick skin.

Knowing that *Daphne Shaw* liked her design made Zoey feel a lot better. Who cared if Ivy thought she looked like a clown if *Daphne Shaw* liked it!

But her readers were right—she did need to learn how to listen to helpful advice. The question was, how did she go about doing that?

She was lying on her bed thinking about that when she suddenly had the inspiration for a new design. Reaching for her sketchbook and pencil,

Zoey started drawing her new idea, inspired by her Sew Zoey readers. *I can't wait to get their constructive criticism on this one,* she thought with a smile.

Zoey was getting a drink at the water fountain between classes the next day when Miles tapped her on the shoulder. She was so surprised, she dribbled water down her shirt.

"You scared me!" she said, wiping her chin with her arm.

"Sorry," Miles said, shifting awkwardly from one foot to the other. Zoey was so used to him being the Goth Kid. Now, instead of standing out, he fit in with everyone else, but Zoey was surprised to realize the preppy look really suited him.

"Can you do me a favor?" he asked. "Can you give this to Priti?"

He held out an envelope with Priti's name on it.

Zoey couldn't understand why he didn't just give it to Priti himself, but she said, "Yeah, okay."

Miles gave her a relieved smile. He really had a very nice smile, Zoey thought. It was something she'd never really noticed when he was dressed in

black all the time—or maybe he just never smiled
that much when he was dressed that way.

"Thanks!" Miles said. "See you later!"

Zoey couldn't wait to find Priti. This was all so
mysterious.

She caught Priti in the hallway during the next
class change and handed her the envelope.

"It's from Miles," she said.

"I wonder what's in it?" Priti said, ripping the
envelope open. She pulled out a letter with a black
necklace taped to it.

"What's this?" she asked, and started reading.

Dear Priti,
We haven't had any time
to hang out since school
started, and I don't have
your phone number so I
figured I'd send you a note.
And this necklace, which
I thought would look really
great on you, because you're
so—

She broke off and started blushing. Priti then grabbed Zoey by the arm and said, *"Come with me to the bathroom!"*

"Why? What is it?" Zoey asked as Priti dragged her down the hallway.

"I need your advice," Priti said.

Now Zoey was even more curious!

As soon as the bathroom door shut behind them, and Priti was sure there was no one else in there, she said, "It's a *love* letter!"

"What?!" Zoey exclaimed. "Wait . . . do you even know each other that well?"

"We hung out during the summer at our sisters' orchestra practices. And part of the reason I started dressing all goth was because I liked the way Miles dressed. But now he's saying . . . Wait, let me read the rest of the letter. . . ."

Priti finished reading what Miles had written, her face flushing even more as she did so.

"I can't believe this, Zo! He says he decided to dress all preppy and have his hair dyed back to its natural color because he wanted me to like him. But then he came back to school and I was dressing like him! We ended up completely swapping styles!"

"No wonder he looked so surprised when he saw you on the first day of school," Zoey said.

"About as surprised as I was to see him," Priti said. "I barely even recognized him!"

That reminded Zoey of a scene from one of her favorite movies. "Oh my gosh, Priti, it's just like in *Grease* when Danny and Sandy liked each other—"

"And swapped styles!" Priti jumped in.

"Sandy traded her poodle skirt for a leather catsuit, and Danny traded his leather jacket for a letterman's cardigan," Zoey recalled, having seen the movie about a thousand times.

"You're right, Zoey," Priti said. "It's a lot like what happened with Miles and me!"

"So . . . do you like him?" Zoey asked. "I mean, you know, *like* like him?"

"I don't know," Priti said. "I'm still in touch with Nick from camp, and I *know* I really like him. But I'm most likely not going to see *him* till next summer. Miles is really nice, but . . . I just *don't know*! I'm not used to having all this attention from boys.

Usually, *I'm* the one with the crush and the other person doesn't like *me*!"

"Well, it seems like Miles is really into you," Zoey said. "What are you going to tell him?"

"I have to think about it," Priti said.

"Don't think for too long," Zoey said. "You can't keep him hanging."

"I know," Priti said. "I always thought it would be fun to have attention from boys, but now I'm not sure I want it."

As Zoey left the bathroom to go to class, she wondered if this love story was going to have a happy ending—or not.

CHAPTER 5

Hip Hippo Hooray!

Thank you to all my awesome Sew Zoey readers for the great advice. I'm definitely going to learn to develop a thicker skin, which is the inspiration for today's design, because (as one of you pointed out) hippos, like elephants and rhinos, are known in the animal kingdom for their incredibly tough hides.

I always thought being creative was all about having fun, but the longer I do Sew Zoey and learn about the business side of designing, the more I realize that there's so much more to it than that. Putting your creations out there in public takes courage—whether it's a clothing design or a poem or a short story or a photograph or a painting. When someone says they don't like your work, it feels so personal, because everything you create contains a little part of you. But if I hadn't started Sew Zoey and kept putting my designs up, so many great things wouldn't have happened. So I'm going to learn to be like a hip hippo and have a thick skin! Now, I just have to figure out how to do it. . . . I guess that's the hard part!

"Hey, Zoey, do you have a minute?" Miles asked in the hall between classes.

It was the Monday after Miles had given Zoey the note to give to Priti.

"Um, yeah, okay," Zoey said, hoping she wasn't going to end up caught in the middle of any awkward love stuff.

"Did you give Priti the envelope?" Miles asked.

"Of course!" Zoey said. "I gave it to her the same day you gave it to me."

"Oh . . . ," Miles said, looking crestfallen. "It's just . . . I haven't heard anything from her. And I noticed she's not wearing the necklace I sent with the letter."

He shifted awkwardly from one foot to the other, glancing down at the floor, then back up at Zoey.

"Did she . . . say anything to you when she read the letter?" he asked.

So much for not being in the middle of any awkward love stuff, Zoey thought.

"I'm not sure what she thinks," she said, which was the truth, because Zoey wasn't sure even *Priti* knew what she thought after reading Miles's letter. "You really should talk to Priti."

"I know." Miles sighed. "I'm just nervous."

"Well, if it makes you feel any better, I think giving her the necklace was really sweet," Zoey said.

"You do?" Miles said, looking considerably cheered up. "Thanks, Zoey."

Zoey just hoped that Priti figured out what she thought by the time Miles talked to her. Otherwise, it was going to be superawkward for both of them.

Later that day, Shannon sidled up to Zoey while she was at her locker, looking around as if she was trying to make sure Ivy and Bree weren't anywhere nearby to observe.

"Hi, Zoey. Hey, can you come over and help me work on some more outfits? Like maybe on Thursday after school?"

Zoey wasn't sure she wanted to go on being Shannon's secret fashion adviser after Shannon had just stood there while Ivy gave her a hard time about her back-to-school outfit.

"I don't know. . . . I'm kind of busy, and—"

"*Please,* Zoey! I got so many compliments on the leopard-print pants outfit you helped me with."

When Zoey still didn't say anything, Shannon said, "I'm sorry about what Ivy said about your outfit. I thought it was cool. . . . It would mean a lot to me if you helped me."

While it felt good to hear Shannon apologize

for Ivy, Zoey still wanted to know why she hadn't done anything to stop Ivy. She was about to ask her when Shannon said, "I've got to go—please say yes."

"Okay. Thursday after school," Zoey relented.

"Great! Thanks, Zo!"

Shannon walked away from her quickly, and not a minute later, was joined by Bree. It made Zoey wish she'd said no instead.

Zoey wished that even more so when Kate called her later that evening wanting to get together after school one day that week.

"How about Wednesday?" she suggested.

"I can't," Zoey said. "Gabe's coming over to take new pictures for the Sew Zoey Etsy site. He thinks some of the new techniques he learned in the photography class he took over the summer might help me get more traffic and sales."

"That's really nice of him," Kate said. "Well, what about Thursday?"

Ack! Zoey thought. *If only I hadn't said yes to Shannon!*

The worst part of saying no to Kate because she'd made plans with Shannon was that because of the promise she'd made to Shannon to keep the whole fashion adviser thing secret, she couldn't be honest with Kate about what she was doing. And that made Zoey feel extra bad about saying no to her.

"I . . . can't. I've got plans."

"Oh . . . okay. Well . . . I have to . . . go. Bye."

Zoey could tell that Kate was upset—again. She sighed as she hung up the phone. Usually, it was Kate who was the one who was busy all the time, running from one practice or game to another. Now that she didn't have those things in her life, she seemed to be taking it really personally that Zoey wasn't available when she wanted to get together.

Recently, there were many awkward situations to try to figure out how to handle! And just when Zoey was getting half excited, half nervous about Gabe coming over to work on the Etsy photographs, she had to worry about how to handle her own awkwardness right now!

Marcus and the members of his band, the Space Invaders, were hanging around in the kitchen on Wednesday afternoon before practice, just before Gabe was scheduled to arrive. Zoey was getting herself a glass of milk.

Her brother couldn't help noticing her hands were shaking when she spilled milk on the counter.

"What's the matter, Zo?" he teased. "Nervous about your boyfriend coming over?"

"Wait? Zoey has a *boyfriend*?" exclaimed Rick, the keyboard player.

"Man, now I feel *ooooold*," Chris, the bass player, groaned. "Zoey's too young to have a boyfriend. She's your little sister."

Zoey blushed.

"He's not my boyfriend," she protested. "He's just a friend who happens to be a boy!"

"'The lady doth protest too much, methinks,'" quoted Dan, the guitar player. "Shakespeare, in case anyone didn't know."

"I don't care who said it, because I'm not protesting too much. I'm telling the truth!" Zoey said, stomping out of the kitchen. She liked her older brother's friends, but sometimes they could be *so annoying!*

After the teasing, Zoey was even more nervous when Gabe rang the doorbell. He was carrying a camera bag, a tripod, and a big nylon disk with differently colored surfaces.

"What's that?" Zoey asked. "It looks like a huge Frisbee."

Gabe laughed. "It does, kind of, but it's called a reflector disk. It's used to reduce shadow," he said. "I'm going to need you to be my assistant and hold it in the right places if I need to use it."

"I think I can handle that," Zoey said.

They went up to Zoey's room, where Zoey had all her most recent designs from the Sew Zoey Etsy store laid out on her worktable.

"I was looking at the clothing on Etsy, and usually, they're on a model," Gabe said.

"I was thinking we could use Marie Antoinette for the model," Zoey said, gesturing to her headless dress form.

Gabe laughed. "Great name for her," he said. "So which outfit is Marie Antoinette going to wear first? Why don't you get her dressed while I set up my stuff and check the lighting?"

After being so nervous before Gabe got there, Zoey wasn't at all nervous once they started working together. She really enjoyed hanging out with him.

"So is Marie Antoinette going to let us eat cake?" Gabe asked after they'd been working for an hour and a half. "I could do with a snack!"

"Sure!" Zoey said. "Although it might have to be cookies. We're not royalty like Marie, so we don't have cake every day."

"I'll just have to slum it," Gabe joked.

They headed down to the kitchen, with the sound of the Space Invaders' band practice in the basement getting louder and louder as they walked down the stairs.

"Is that your brother's band?" Gabe asked.

"Yeah, the Space Invaders."

"They're good," Gabe said.

"I know," Zoey said. She *was* proud of Marcus,

and the success of his band. "But they can also be kind of annoying at times. It's like having your older brother multiplied by four."

"That could have its pros and cons, definitely," Gabe said, smiling.

Zoey got out some cookies and milk, and they sat on the kitchen stools to snack.

"It's so nice of you to take the pictures, Gabe," Zoey said. "They look much better. I'll let you know what happens with the traffic and sales after I upload them."

"Cool," Gabe said. "It'll be interesting to see."

"Can I do something to help you out?" Zoey asked. "Like maybe I could make you a special outfit or help you with a photo project or something? As you can see, I'm a great assistant. I can hold the photo Frisbee reflector thingy like a pro!"

Gabe laughed. "You're a total Frisbee-reflector-thingy-holder expert. No doubt about it," he said. "But, actually, I have a better idea. I have a photo project due next week, and I need a subject. You'd be perfect for it. What do you think?"

"A subject . . . You mean, like a model?" Zoey asked. "I don't know."

"C'mon, it'll be fun," Gabe said. "How about this Sunday?"

"Okay," Zoey said. Even though modeling wasn't really her thing, she wanted to spend more time with Gabe. They could joke around and be goofy together, and he seemed to really get her. When she stopped to think about it, the fact that he asked her to be his photo subject made her happy, because it meant he probably enjoyed spending time with her, too.

CHAPTER 6

New Look

Thanks to my friend Gabe, my Etsy site has a new look, with great pictures that show off the clothes so much better. He took a photography class over the summer when I was taking screen-printing, and he learned about lighting and different digital effects and filters.

When you look at things through a different lens, it's amazing how it can change your perception of what you're looking at. It can make an object look completely different. It's kind of like that with people, too. You can think about them one way and then see them in a different light. I guess it pays to keep your eyes and your mind open, right?

The next evening, Marcus dropped Zoey off at Shannon's house, so she could help her with more fashion advice.

"So when did you and Shannon start getting all *buddy-buddy* again?" Marcus asked.

"We're not exactly *buddy-buddy*," Zoey said. "In fact, I'm not sure what we are. I said I'd help her pick some more outfits, that's all."

"Oh. Well, have fun," Marcus said.

Zoey wasn't sure if it was going to be fun or not.

One thing *was* sure—Daisy was very excited to see her again.

"Zoey's here! Zoey's here!" she shouted up to Shannon, dancing around at the bottom of the stairs as Zoey made her way to the kitchen.

"Daisy *loved* the outfit you made for Sophie Flynn," Mrs. Chang said, filling the teakettle up with water at the sink. "She thought it was so cool that you made it especially for her."

"It was *awesome!*" Daisy exclaimed, running into the kitchen and throwing her arms around Zoey's waist. "I asked Shannon if she could ask you to make one for me." She looked up at Zoey with adoring brown eyes. "How come you stopped coming over to hang out?"

Shannon, who'd just come into the kitchen and heard the question, said, "Daisy! Hush up!"

Daisy dropped her arms from around Zoey's waist and looked at her sister defiantly. "I just want to know why! I miss seeing Zoey!"

"*Mommmmm!*" Shannon yelled, but Mrs. Chang was busy with the teakettle, leaving Shannon to answer the question herself.

"I'm not sure . . . ," Shannon said, clearly feeling awkward about the situation. "But . . . I'd like us to start hanging out more again."

"Good," Daisy said.

Zoey was surprised by how much Daisy seemed to miss her—and what Shannon said. She wondered if Shannon really meant it and if she would be willing to hang out with her in public, or if hanging out was another thing she was supposed to keep under wraps.

"I'd be happy to make an outfit for you, Daisy, but I can't do it right away. I have to make one for a friend of mine first," Zoey explained.

Daisy looked disappointed, but Mrs. Chang said, "That's very generous of you, Zoey. Daisy can wait until you have time, can't you, Daisy?"

"I guess," Daisy said. "Thanks, Zoey."

"Come on, Zoey, let's go upstairs," Shannon said, anxious to get away before Daisy could ask any more awkward questions.

In Shannon's room, Zoey sifted through her closet, pulling out pieces to put together into new combinations of outfits for her to try on. After an hour and a half, they had enough outfits to keep Shannon going for at least the next quarter.

"How do you do it?" Shannon asked. "I see these clothes all the time, but I never think of putting them together the way you do. It's kind of amazing."

"I'm not sure," Zoey said. "I just have a knack for it, I guess."

"I really appreciate you coming over," Shannon said. "In case you couldn't guess, Daisy's been talking about you nonstop since the last time you were here."

Zoey was just about to ask Shannon if things were going to be any different at school when Mrs. Chang called up to say Zoey's father had arrived to pick her up. She'd have to save her question for another time.

Zoey brought her sketchbook to school the next day to show Priti the outfit she'd decided to design to support Priti's new look—an all-black dress, complete with black lace and rivets.

"I love it!" Priti said. "I can't tell you how happy it makes me, especially now."

"Why especially now?" Zoey asked.

"Because my parents *hate*, and I mean seriously hate, my new look, and they've told me I can't buy any more black clothes," Priti explained. "It's the only thing they've agreed on in months. What's even worse is that they've forbidden me to wear any of my black outfits to school."

Zoey stared at Priti. She was dressed from top to toe in black, just like she'd been every day since school started.

"Um . . . so . . ." Zoey looked pointedly at Priti's black ensemble.

"Oh . . . yeah. Well, I've been bringing the clothes I *want* to wear in my backpack and changing in the bathroom when I get to school," Priti said sheepishly. "My parents are making all the other decisions in my life without giving me a say, so shouldn't I at least be able to pick what I get to wear?"

Zoey didn't like the idea of disobeying her parents, but on the other hand, her dad hadn't ever forbidden her from wearing the clothes she wanted to wear. And she'd never had to go through her parents getting divorced. She couldn't imagine what it must be like.

"Seems fair to me, but what happens if they find out?"

"I'll worry about that if they do," Priti said. "But

I know Libby and Kate feel the same way about my look as Mom and Dad, so I'm extra-specially grateful that you're being so supportive."

"Hey, I'm all about experimenting with new ideas and looks. After the first-day-of-school outfit, I'm learning how to deal with what happens when I don't pull them off," Zoey said.

Priti laughed. "It wasn't *that* bad."

"Thanks, but it wasn't my most successful look either," Zoey said. "But that's okay. Not everyone's going to like everything I design. I'm just glad you like this!"

At lunch, Kate told her friends that whatever excitement she'd felt about taking piano lessons was well and truly gone. She hated the piano.

"I seriously wish I'd broken my fingers instead of hurt my elbow," she complained. "Then I wouldn't have to take lessons anymore."

"Why don't you just tell your mom how much you hate it?" Priti suggested. "Tell her you want to stop taking lessons."

"I tried that." Kate sighed. "She just insists I

stick with it because no one learns how to play an instrument overnight. Even worse, she starts telling me how disappointed she is that I would want to give up so quickly, because I've never shown signs of being a quitter on the sports field."

"But you love sports," Libby said. "Maybe you just don't love piano."

"I know!" Kate said. "I tried telling her that sports are my thing and that's why I love them. But Mom says that piano talent runs in our family, so she's sure I have musical talent hidden inside." She sighed again. "All I can say is that it must be hidden very *deep* inside, because I don't see any sign of it. Neither does my piano teacher, from what I can tell."

"Maybe if you keep at it for a little longer and you're still miserable, you can try talking to her again," Zoey suggested.

"I just hope the doctor says I can go back to playing sports soon," Kate said. "Because it stinks not being able to do what I really enjoy."

Zoey could understand that. She hoped Kate could get back to sports again soon, too.

Ever since the photo session with Gabe on Wednesday, Zoey had been looking forward to meeting up with him again on Sunday to pose for his photography project. They met at the public library.

"My idea was to shoot you in interesting poses by the statues in the courtyard," Gabe said.

"Um . . . what do you mean by interesting poses?" Zoey asked.

"Just have fun with it, Zoey," Gabe said. "You're *always* interesting!"

Zoey smiled. Being interesting was a good thing, right?

Once again, Zoey had a great time hanging out with Gabe. They made each other laugh, and Gabe encouraged Zoey to be dramatic and then silly, so he could get different looks and facial expressions.

"You're a great subject," Gabe said when they were finished and waiting to be picked up. "I'll have to use you for another photo project."

Marcus pulled up then.

"Any time. It was fun," Zoey said. "See you in school tomorrow!"

When Zoey did see Gabe in school later that week, she mentioned getting together again on Thursday.

"Oh, yeah. I can't. I'm . . . um . . . really busy this week," he said, blushing slightly.

"Okay," Zoey said. "Maybe next week, then."

"Yeah, maybe," Gabe said.

"When's good for you?" Zoey asked.

"I don't know yet. Let's see how it goes." He didn't quite meet her eyes.

Zoey was confused. She really enjoyed hanging out with Gabe, and she thought he enjoyed hanging out with her. She'd also thought he'd had a crush on her, especially after what he'd written in her yearbook at the end of last year.

But now that she wanted to hang out with him, he didn't seem to want to hang out with her so much. She liked Gabe the more she got to know him, but maybe he didn't feel the same way. Did Gabe like the *idea* of Zoey more than *actual* Zoey?

CHAPTER 7

Got Goth?

Even though I'm still not 100 percent used to seeing Priti, the queen of color and sparkle, dressing in black every day, I want to support her the way she always supports me. So I designed her a superfab lace-and-rivets outfit of her very own. I threw in a few black sparkles around the neckline just for fun—and because I believe that somewhere inside, Colorful and Sparkly Priti is still there under all the dark clothing. Maybe I'll convince her to accessorize with a splash of color on the outside, too, once in a while. Or maybe we can go to the Perfect Ten for a mani-pedi, and she can get colorful fingers and toes. I mean, we all need a little bit of color in our lives, don't we?

Am I being too critical for wanting to see a little color on Priti's fingers and toes when she's totally into the all-black thing? I want to be a good friend. It's just weird to see her looking so different from the Priti we know and love. But we'll get used to it, I'm sure.

Zoey was feeling a little glum the following week when she got home from school. Gabe was still being evasive about getting together. She'd noticed he was spending a lot of time with Josie. But maybe that was just because he wanted to practice speaking French. She'd even seen them sitting together at lunch, though there were other people at the table too.

She quickly scanned her Sew Zoey comments and then checked her e-mail before starting on her homework. One name in her in-box leaped out at her.

Bryn Allen!

Bryn Allen was the teenage star of *So Chill*, one of Zoey's favorite sitcoms. When she opened the e-mail and read it, Zoey forgot that she'd been feeling down.

Hey, Sew Zoey,

Hope you don't mind me e-mailing you out of the blue, but I saw the sketch you did of that adorable goth outfit, and I was wondering if you could make me one for an event I'm going to in a few weeks. Is it too much of a rush job, or can you handle it?

Let me know,

Bryn Allen

I can't believe it! Zoey thought. *A TV star wants to wear one of my designs!*

But then she realized that to get the outfit

ready for *Bryn Allen* to wear in a few weeks, she'd have to put off the work on the outfit she was making for Priti. Her friend was having such a tough time lately, having to face the disappointment that her parents weren't going to get back together and having to get used to her new life of shuttling back and forth between their two houses. Zoey didn't want to add any more disappointment to Priti's list. But how could she possibly refuse a request from Bryn Allen? Making something for her would be amazing exposure for Sew Zoey and also just plain exciting.

She waited until lunch the next day to tell her friends.

"I need your help with something," she said. "I got an e-mail last night from Bryn Allen."

"Wait . . . you mean THE BRYN ALLEN? The *actress*?" Priti exclaimed.

Zoey nodded.

"The star of So *Chill*?" Libby asked.

"That's the one," Zoey confirmed.

"Wow!" Kate exclaimed. "What does she want?"

"She saw the outfit I designed for Priti on my

blog, and she wants me to make her one just like it for an event she's going to," Zoey said.

"That's incredible!" Libby said. "Think of all the publicity you'll get if some magazine prints a picture of her wearing your outfit!"

"I know," Zoey said. "It's just . . . the event is in a few weeks, and, Priti, I promised you that I'd make yours. I'd have to put yours on hold to get the one for Bryn done in time."

"Have you gone *totally cray*?" Priti said. "Of course you should do the one for Bryn!"

"Are you sure?" Zoey asked.

"Totally sure," Priti said. "I mean, sure, I was looking forward to wearing the outfit, but you can just make mine as soon as you can after you finish the one for Bryn, right?"

"Definitely," Zoey assured her. "And I'll make hers as fast as I can—so I'm hoping it won't take too long."

"Now Priti can say that Bryn Allen copied *her* look," Kate said with a laugh.

"That's right!" Zoey said. "Priti Holbrooke, trendsetter."

Priti preened. "That's me, girlfriends! Just follow my fashion lead."

Kate and Libby exchanged dubious glances. They definitely weren't ready to follow Priti's lead of wearing all black. Not yet. Maybe not ever!

"I can't wait to go home and e-mail Bryn Allen back," Zoey told Libby as they walked to class after lunch.

"I know," Libby said. "It's so exciting that she even reads your blog, let alone wants you to make her an outfit."

"Maybe I'll get to meet her," Zoey said. "I mean for fittings and stuff, and—"

She broke off, distracted by the sight of Gabe and Josie walking down the hallway, holding hands and smiling at each other. Zoey felt her heart contract as she suddenly realized the reason why Gabe never seemed to be available anymore. Then she realized that she was jealous, and the force of it surprised her.

"I can't believe Gabe is holding hands with Josie," she complained to Libby. "We've had so much fun hanging out together recently. I thought he liked *me*."

"Zo, you never admitted to *like* liking Gabe until now, when you've suddenly seen him with someone else," Libby said. "Are you sure it's not just that you're suddenly liking him because he's taken?"

"What?" Zoey said. "I don't think so. I mean . . ."

She'd have to think about that. She'd always liked Gabe as a friend, but was it just because he was always there to help out or because she really *liked* liked him?

"I don't know," she admitted.

"Think about it," Libby suggested. "Hopefully, you didn't figure out you like him just as he figured out he likes Josie. Because that would stink."

Later in the day, Zoey caught up with Gabe between classes—this time, he was alone.

"Hi, Gabe," she said.

"Oh, hi, Zoey!" he said, greeting her with a warm, friendly smile. "How's it going? Everything good with the website?"

"I've noticed an increase in page views since I put up the new pictures," Zoey said. "But it's the early days."

"Great!" he said. "I was pretty sure new pictures would help."

"How did the project go?"

"I got an A," Gabe said with a grin. "I'm pretty sure that's because I had such an awesome subject."

He was being so adorable and friendly that Zoey wondered if maybe he did like her after all. But then she remembered the hand holding with Josie in the hallway. She decided to just be straightforward and ask him.

"So . . . what's going on with you and Josie?"

"What do you mean?"

"Are you going out or something?"

"Not really—she's a nice girl, though," Gabe said. "It's interesting to hear about living in Paris."

Zoey didn't understand why he'd be holding hands with Josie if they weren't going out. And Gabe's eyes lit up when he spoke about Josie. Zoey went to her next class feeling even more insecure about the whole thing. Boys could be so confusing!

It turned out Zoey wasn't the only one feeling confused and insecure. When she finally got together with Kate over the weekend, her friend expressed similar feelings.

"You never seem to have time to get together anymore. You're spending a lot of time with Shannon, and when you do, you don't want me to hang out with you. Or else you're hanging out with Gabe, and then it's the same thing," Kate complained.

"I'm sorry," Zoey said. "It's just that . . ."

Ack! Problem. She couldn't tell Kate why she wasn't able to invite her to join her and Shannon because she'd promised to keep it a secret. That promise was getting to be seriously annoying!

"It's just that I've been busy," she continued, realizing that it sounded like she was making excuses again. But at least she could be honest with Kate about Gabe.

"And to tell you the truth, the reason I didn't invite you to join in when I hung out with Gabe is because, well, I thought I was starting to get a crush on him. Well, I am kind of getting a crush on him. But now I think he has a crush on Josie."

"Oh, Zoey," Kate said, immediately sympathetic.

"The thing is, I like Josie. She's really nice. And I like Gabe. And I'm not sure if the reason I'm so upset is just because he suddenly likes someone else or because I really like him."

"Guys are so confusing," Kate said. "That's why I like sports. The rules are the rules, so you know what's what."

"That's why I like sewing," Zoey said. "Because if I make a mistake, I can just rip out the stitches and do it over. It's harder to do it over with people."

"I'm glad you're not ripping *me* out of your life," Kate said.

"No way," Zoey said. "We're BFFs. And when I say best friends forever, I really *mean* forever!"

CHAPTER 8

Which Way, Weather Vane?

Do you ever feel torn in lots of different directions? That's the feeling that inspired today's designs. Some of the directions are exciting—like when someone famous (!!!) sees a design on your website and wants you to make it for her (!!!!!!!!!!!!!!!!!! ☺), but then you feel bad because you're not working on the one for your friend and you aren't spending enough time with your other friends and soooo . . . you end up feeling like you don't know which way to turn first.

Even though it's all good, sometimes I wish the weather vane would stop spinning for a day or two, so I could just chill. Is this part of growing up? If so, I'm not sure I'm ready.

When Zoey e-mailed back Bryn Allen, Bryn's response was really enthusiastic. She wrote:

> I'm so psyched you're on board to make my outfit. I can't wait to wear it! I look forward to meeting you in person when I come for the fitting.
> Cheers, Bryn

Bryn included her measurements in the e-mail too.

Come for the fitting?! Bryn Allen come to her house? A real-life TV star? Zoey had only imagined that possibility. But now she had an e-mail from

Bryn saying it was really going to happen!

"Dad! Dad! Guess what!" she shouted, racing downstairs to the kitchen where her father was making dinner.

"Well, judging by the excited shouting, I'm guessing either we won the lottery or that it's something exciting to do with Sew Zoey," her dad said.

"The second one!" Zoey said. "Bryn Allen liked the outfit I designed for Priti, and she wants me to make her one to wear to some event, and she's going to *come to our house for a fitting*!"

"Wait, you mean Bryn Allen from *So Chill*?" Marcus asked.

"Yes!" Zoey exclaimed.

"Wow," Marcus said. "She's famous. Like having her picture in *Celebrity* magazine famous."

"Well, I can tell you one thing," Dad said, "and that's that we're all going to do some major cleaning before any famous TV star sets foot in this house. We've got to make a good impression."

"Between sewing and housecleaning, I'm going to be working nonstop!" Zoey complained.

But work nonstop she did. She came straight home from school every day, did her homework, then focused on Bryn's outfit, so she could get it ready in time for the fitting appointment she'd arranged with Bryn that weekend.

Of course, Bryn's imminent arrival at Casa Webber meant Zoey, Marcus, and Dad spent part of every evening cleaning, too, so that the house looked spotless before she arrived.

"I don't think the house has been this clean before, ever," Marcus said.

"Maybe not since the day we moved in," Dad joked.

"She's going to think we're freaks," Zoey said. "The whole house smells like cleaning products."

"I know. It's unnatural," Marcus complained. "We need to get Aunt Lulu to bring Buttons over, so at least there's something normal about our house, like dog hair on the carpet."

"No way!" Dad exclaimed. "Not after I just vacuumed! No dog hair till *after* the star visits!"

Zoey and Marcus exchanged looks.

"Who knew Dad was such a Martha Stewart?"

Marcus sighed. "It's a good thing we don't have TV stars visiting every day. He'd be totally impossible to live with!"

On the day of the fitting, Zoey was beside herself with excitement. Marcus's girlfriend, Allie, came over because she was a huge fan of Bryn's, and she was as excited as Zoey.

"Do you think she's as funny in person as she is on TV?" Allie asked.

"Who knows?" Marcus said. "When she's on TV, she's just performing from a script."

"I bet she's funny," Zoey said. "That can't *all* be acting."

"But that's why it's called acting, Zo!" Marcus pointed out. "Because you're being something you're not."

"I still think she's funny in real life, too," Zoey said. "She has to be."

"We'll see," Marcus said.

Zoey threw a sofa cushion at him for being such a grump.

"Stop it, Zo! Dad will have a hissy fit because

you're ruining our perfect home impression!" Marcus joked.

The doorbell rang.

"*Oh my gosh*! That must be her!" Zoey squealed. "Quick! Put the cushion back in place!"

"*Argh*. Zoey's getting as bad as Dad," Marcus said, groaning. "I'm going to have to move if this keeps up."

She ran to open the front door.

Bryn Allen—*the* Bryn Allen—stood on the doorstep.

"Hi—Zoey?" she said.

"Yes! You look the same as you do on TV!" Zoey said. And then she blushed because she'd planned to play it cool and professional, but she hadn't exactly gotten off to a great start.

Fortunately, Bryn just laughed.

"Funny how that works—because it's plain old me who is *on* TV," she said.

Then they both laughed, and Zoey felt less silly.

"Come on in," she said.

"I love your house," Bryn said as they walked inside. "It's so . . . neat. My house is a total mess."

Zoey giggled. "It's not normally this neat. Dad made us clean up to make a good impression on you."

Bryn smiled. "Tell your dad it was worth it. I am *seriously*, *very* impressed."

Marcus wasn't a big watcher of teen-girl shows, so he took meeting Bryn in stride. But Allie was a different story.

"Hi . . . I'm . . . A-Allie," she stammered. "I'm a huge f-fan."

Allie was normally so confident and articulate. Zoey couldn't believe how starstruck she was all of a sudden—even worse than Zoey was!

"Hi, Allie! Great to meet you!" Bryn said.

"Allie makes really great accessories," Zoey said, figuring if she got Allie talking about her work, she'd be less nervous. "She brought some over to show you."

"I th-thought you could pick something you like—I mean, only if you want to, that is," Allie said. "You don't have to."

Bryn looked over the accessories Allie had displayed on the table.

"I'd love to pick something," she exclaimed. "The problem is deciding what to pick! They're all so cool."

Allie smiled, visibly relaxing a little.

"You can take more than one, if you'd like," she said. "I love your show so much, it's the least I can do."

Bryn picked out an adorable embroidered purse and a hair accessory.

"Are you sure you don't want me to pay you?" she said.

"Oh, no," Allie insisted. "They're a gift. But . . . can we take a picture together, so I can show my friends I met you?"

"Definitely," Bryn said.

She hugged Allie, and Marcus took a picture of them together.

"My friends are going to be so jealous!" Allie said. "Keep up the great work!"

"We'd better get on with the fitting," Zoey said. "Otherwise, I'm not going to get *my* work done in time for your event."

She and Bryn went up to Zoey's room where Bryn's outfit was being modeled by Marie Antoinette.

"What do you think?" Zoey asked.

Bryn looked around and said, "I love your room! It's so homey. I spend so much time in hotels and TV-show trailers. It must be great knowing you get to spend every night in your own cozy room."

"I guess," Zoey said. "But it must be pretty awesome to be on TV, too."

"Oh, it is," Bryn said. "I love what I do. But sometimes I miss being just a regular girl, you know what I mean?"

Zoey could only imagine. But to her, Bryn seemed like a regular girl who just happened to be a big TV star.

"What about the outfit?" she said, gesturing to Marie Antoinette. "What do you think so far?"

"I love it!" Bryn said. "I can't wait to try it on!"

"Let's do it," Zoey said.

When Bryn was in the outfit, Zoey pinned and marked for the alterations she would need to make.

Bryn kept cracking jokes the whole time, making Zoey laugh so hard, she was afraid she was going to stick her with straight pins by mistake. She could just imagine the *Celebrity* magazine story: "TV star turned into a pincushion by giggling seamstress."

"You know, I was thinking . . . ," Bryn mused, finally taking a break from the jests. "What if we put a few more rivets here? I think that would look really cool."

"I could do that," Zoey said.

"And maybe add a little more lace around the edge here?" Bryn suggested.

"Um . . . sure," Zoey said, taking notes and marking on the fabric.

By the time Bryn had finished, Zoey had a list of little changes Bryn wanted made to the outfit, which added up to quite a bit of extra work beyond fitting for size.

"So when should I come back for the next fitting?" Bryn asked. "The event is next week."

Zoey looked at the list and wondered how she was going to get it all done. She *had* to get it all done. She was a professional, and this was a big break!

"Give me a few days," she said.

"Great, I'll be back in two days," Bryn said. "It's so much fun working with you, Zoey. It's like hanging out with a friend!"

As soon as Bryn left, Zoey got straight to work on the alterations. She was busy adding the new rivets when Kate dropped by.

"What was Bryn Allen like?" Kate asked.

"She's really nice," Zoey said. "It's like she's just a normal girl, like you and me, but also a star. And she's as funny in real life as she is on TV."

"That's cool," Kate said. "I always imagine stars are different somehow—like they come from another planet."

"That's the *other* kind of star," Zoey joked.

"Ha, ha!" Kate laughed. "So I was thinking, do you want to go to the movies? Everyone says the new one at the Main Street Cinema is really great, and there's a show at three."

Zoey hated to have to say no to Kate *again*. But she knew she needed all the time she had to spare to finish the alterations for Bryn in time.

"I can't," she said.

Kate's face showed her disappointment.

"It's not that I don't *want* to," Zoey rushed to explain. "Bryn asked me for lots of little changes to her outfit, and I have to get those done, plus the regular alterations, before she comes back in two days."

"I understand," Kate said. "Well, I don't want to hold you up from your work. I'll see you later, Zo."

As she went back to work on Bryn's outfit, Zoey felt torn. She missed hanging out with Kate and felt bad that every time Kate asked to get together, the answer was always no. She knew Kate was upset with her, and she hated upsetting one of her best friends. Why was it always so hard to get everything done *and* keep everyone happy?

CHAPTER 9

Starstruck

You know what's so cool? When you meet someone famous and you expect them to be totally different from you, because, you know they're famous and on TV, but actually they're really down-to-earth and cool. That's what it was like meeting . . . BRYN ALLEN (!!!) when she came to our house for a fitting. I know! Bryn Allen was in our house! I can hardly believe it myself. Even Dad was freaking out, making us clean like crazy. But Bryn was so nice—and really funny. And she's coming back in a few days for another fitting. I think I have to pinch myself!

In the meantime, I'm just work, work, working to make sure I get everything done. I just hope all work and no play doesn't make me a dull girl. Or worse yet, a bad friend . . .

When Priti showed up at school that following Monday after Bryn's fitting, Zoey was shocked to see her dressed in "former Priti" style—brightly colored clothes with sparkly accent accessories. Zoey'd gotten so used to seeing her friend in her new dark look that she wondered what happened.

Kate and Libby, however, were thrilled.

"Priti! It's so great to see you looking like yourself again!" Libby exclaimed.

"I know, right?" Kate agreed. "Color suits you so much better."

Priti regarded her friends in awkward silence.

"I'm not wearing these clothes by choice," she said finally. "I don't *want* to dress this way. It might be how you see me, but it's not how *I* see me right now."

"What happened?" Zoey asked. "Why *are* you wearing your old clothes?"

"My mom went to put a treat from her food blog into my backpack last night as a surprise," Priti said with a sigh. "And she found the black outfit I'd packed to change into today at school. She got really mad and asked me if I was wearing all-black outfits to school, even though she and my dad told me I wasn't allowed."

"Oh no!" Libby exclaimed. "What did you do?"

"I told her the truth," Priti said. "I said that I like dressing in black, and I can't understand why she and Dad hate it so much. It's the only thing Mom and Dad have actually *agreed on* in, like, *forever*, which, to tell you the truth, is something that makes me want to do it even more."

"Wow. How did she take that?" Kate asked.

"Well, she was mad at first. But eventually she calmed down, and we talked some more. She told me why she didn't like me dressing in all black, and I told her that since she and Dad are making all these major changes in my life without me getting to have a say, the least they can do is let me choose what I wear," Priti explained. "And after she had a chance to think about it, she said she was willing to go along with my fashion decisions. But she has to talk to Dad about it first."

"That's great!" Zoey said. "It sounds like your mom is listening to you."

"It felt like that for the first time in a while," Priti admitted. "I just hope she talks to Dad soon, so I can go back to wearing what I want to wear. I feel out of sorts wearing these clothes. They just aren't me anymore. Or at least right now, anyway."

"I'm sorry for not understanding about your new outfits," Libby said.

"Me too," Kate added. "It's not that I don't like them. It's just . . ."

"It's just that we miss colorful, sparkly Priti," Libby explained.

"That's right," Kate said. "The Priti whose fashion philosophy is 'more color, more sparkle!'"

"She's still there, inside," Priti assured them. "I'm still the same Priti—I'm just wearing different clothes, that's all."

When Bryn came for her second fitting, Allie, who was over at the house, hanging out with Marcus, was more relaxed and less tongue-tied.

"Hey, Bryn," she said from the sofa, where she and Marcus were watching a movie. "How are things in TV Land?"

"Pretty good," Bryn said. She pointed to the bowl of popcorn and empty glasses on the table in front of them.

"I see your dad has chilled about keeping up the perfect house image," she observed, smiling.

"Oh, yeah." Marcus laughed. "You only get the special star-cleaning package on your first visit. It's all downhill from here."

"Good," Bryn said. "It makes me feel more comfortable and at home if there's at least *some* messiness."

She and Zoey went up to Zoey's room to try on the altered outfit.

It fit Bryn perfectly, but once again, she had lots of ideas for little changes she wanted.

"Could we just tweak this a little bit here, like this?" she asked, gathering the fabric at the bodice.

"And then could we adjust this here just a tad?"

"And maybe do this?"

Zoey's cell rang. It was Kate.

"Excuse me a minute," Zoey said, not wanting to let it go to voice mail.

"Hi, Kate," she said. "I can't talk now because I'm in the middle of Bryn's fitting, but why don't you come over?"

"Okay, great!" Kate exclaimed. "I can't wait to meet her!"

"I hope it's okay if my friend Kate comes over to meet you," Zoey said after she hung up. "She's a big fan of yours. And it's been hard because we haven't had so much time to hang out recently."

"No problem. I know how that is," Bryn said. "Balancing work and friendship gets complicated sometimes."

And then she made a request for *another* "little" change. Zoey's list was getting longer and longer.

As Zoey took notes and pinned all the adjust-ments, she worried that she was never going to finish Bryn's outfit and be able to start on Priti's if Bryn kept on like this. Not only that, the outfit was starting to look less and less like the one she designed and more like something . . . well, com-pletely different.

Kate was excited to meet Bryn, and Zoey took a picture of the two of them together once Bryn had changed back into her regular clothes.

"It's so great that you guys live so close to each other," Bryn said, as she was leaving. "It makes it easy to hang out all the time."

"Not that easy," Kate muttered.

Zoey knew she had to get to work on the altera-tions for Bryn, but she also knew she had to talk to Kate.

"Let's go have a snack," she said after Bryn left.

Over cookies and milk, she apologized to Kate for not hanging out as much as she'd like.

"I know you said not to worry, but between Shannon, Gabe, and now your famous new friend, Bryn, it feels like you're slipping away from me,"

Kate confessed. "We've been friends forever—as long as I can remember. I just thought that now that I have time after school, we'd be able to hang out more."

"I know," Zoey said. "But see . . . this is how my life has been since starting Sew Zoey and all my different sewing projects. I always seem to be crazy busy with one thing or another. The thing is, you usually don't notice because you're so crazy busy with sports."

"I guess," Kate admitted.

"I can't just drop everything because now you have free time," Zoey said. "But I swear, it's not because I'm trying to push you away or anything like that. So, please, don't take it personally, okay?"

"I'll try," Kate said. "I'll really try."

But on the bus ride going home from school the next day, Zoey asked Kate what she was up to the coming weekend.

"Nothing much," Kate said. "But I'm not going to ask about getting together because I know you're really busy."

Zoey didn't know what to say. She *was* busy. She still had lots of alterations to get done for Bryn's outfit, and not much time to do them. But she hated to see her friend's feelings so hurt, and she didn't know what to do about it.

That night, she explained the situation to her dad.

"Since she can't do sports, Kate's taking piano lessons, but she hates them, and when she's not doing that, she wants to hang out all the time, but I can't because I'm busy with the stuff I'm doing for Sew Zoey," she said. "How do I balance it all? I have to do my work to keep Bryn happy, but I want to be a good friend, too."

"Well, Zo, I've been thinking that maybe you should spread your creative wings a bit—you know, all work and no play makes Zoey a dull, stressed-out girl and stuff," he said. "I know you love sewing and blogging, but there might be other things you love too if you give them a chance."

"Like what?" Zoey asked.

"I don't know yet," Dad said. "But I'm thinking we might be able to kill two birds with one stone here. I could talk to Mrs. Mackey and suggest that you and Kate figure out a class you might take together—preferably something that involves movement, since you spend a lot of time sitting when you're sewing and blogging, and I think that's something Kate misses right now."

"But when will I have time?" Zoey asked, already feeling stressed about it. "I'm so busy!"

"You can spare one night a week," Dad said. "And this way, you'll get to spend time with Kate, doing something fun."

Kate loved the idea, and started looking into different alternatives that would be fun for both of them and would incorporate movement but not so much movement that it would put strain on her elbow.

"Well, yoga is out," she told Zoey on the bus. "That's too bad. That would be fun. Pottery looks fun, but I can't use my arm for that."

"And that's more sitting, not moving," Zoey said. "Dad wants me to move."

"I'll keep looking," Kate said. "We've got to be able to find *something* that works for both of us."

That night, Zoey popped her head into the living room to talk to her dad, who was channel surfing to see what was on.

"Wait!" she said. "Go back a few channels!"

Her father changed the channel back, and there on the screen were three people, dancing and singing. Not just dancing. *Tap dancing*. It looked like *so much fun!*

"*That's* what I want to do!" Zoey exclaimed.

"*Singin' in the Rain*?" her dad said.

"No, *tap dancing*!" Zoey said. "I have to call Kate!"

Kate loved the idea. "It'll be so much fun!" she said. "Mom says she just has to check with the instructor and my doctor tomorrow to make sure that the moves can be modified so they won't hurt my elbow."

"Let's hope they say yes!" Zoey said.

As soon as she hung up, she grabbed her sketchbook and, inspired by thoughts of tap dancing with her friend, she started drawing.

CHAPTER 10

Tap to Toe

Watch out, world! Kate and I are going to be doing a happy dance! Yes, inspired by the classic movie *Singin' in the Rain*, we're going to take tap lessons, and to celebrate, I designed these sparkly clips for our tap shoes. Wouldn't they look great with these accessories?

It'll be fun to try something new—like Dad said, it's good for me to spread my creative wings—but mostly I'm excited to hang out with Kate. Just you wait . . . We're going to wow everyone at the talent show after this!

Now if I can just get all of Bryn Allen's alterations done in time . . . Back to work!

"I'm so excited for our first tap class!" Kate said as Mrs. Mackey dropped them off the following evening.

Mrs. Mackey had approval from Kate's doctor, as long as Kate was careful not to fall and she kept her arm in her sling, so she didn't make any wild arm movements that might damage her elbow. She had also called the dancing instructor, who explained that the beginning class focused mostly on footwork.

"I am too!" Zoey said. "I'm glad we're doing this together."

Zoey thought tap class was a blast. She loved dancing, and it turned out she had a knack for tap. It also felt good to be doing something besides being hunched over her sewing table working on yet *another* of the changes Bryn had requested for her outfit.

Kate wasn't quite as enamored of their shared pastime. She found it frustrating.

"It was fun—especially being with Zoey—but it doesn't come naturally to me the way like, say, swimming or soccer does," she told her friends at lunch the next day. "I have to really *work* at it."

"You have to try and *feel* the music," Priti said. "And then just move with it. It's more important to do that than to get every single step perfect, I think."

"But I'm not used to *feeling music*," Kate complained. "I'm better at reacting to opponents' moves, or defending the ball."

"I'm sure you'll get the hang of it eventually," Libby said.

"I hope so," Kate said. "Because that's what Mom said about piano lessons, and *that* hasn't happened. But anyway . . . I'm having fun hanging out with Zoey, so it's already a win, no matter what happens!"

By the time Bryn came for her next fitting on Sunday, the stars in Zoey's eyes had already begun to fade. She really liked Bryn, but it was frustrating how Bryn kept changing the design when Zoey thought she was finished.

"Is it okay to get this frustrated with a famous person?" Zoey asked her father and Marcus the night before the fitting. "I mean, isn't she doing me a favor by buying one of my designs?"

"It's okay to get frustrated with anyone who behaves toward you in an inconsiderate way, whether they're famous or not," Dad said.

"You're doing *her* a favor by making her such a cool outfit," Marcus said. "You should tell her she's got to finalize the design, and that's it."

"Yeah," Zoey said. "I guess I need to say something to her when she comes."

She knew they were right, but she wasn't looking forward to the conversation. Not one little bit.

When Bryn arrived for her fitting on Saturday, Zoey tried to gather up her courage to say something.

It was hard because she really liked Bryn, and she didn't want to upset her.

"I really love how it's looking," Bryn said when she saw the outfit. "I was just thinking . . . if we could take put a little extra lace here . . . What do you think?"

Zoey took a deep breath.

"I think we need to finalize the design, Bryn," she said. "The thing is, I can't make any more alterations. I've already spent a lot more time on this than I'd budgeted because of all the changes you asked for. I want you to be happy with the outfit, but . . ."

She trailed off, seeing the expression on Bryn's face. She wasn't happy. Not happy at all.

"Fine," she said. "I guess we're done, then!"

And she turned on her heel and stomped out of the room.

"Wait, Bryn, I . . . ," Zoey called after her. She ran to see if she could catch Bryn, but it was too late. She heard the front door slam, and by the time Zoey got there to open it and look out, she saw the taillights of Bryn's limousine heading down the street.

"Great." She sighed. "Now I've totally blown it."

Dad and Marcus, who'd heard the door slam too, came to investigate what happened.

"I gather Bryn didn't take the conversation too well," Dad said.

"That's an understatement," Zoey said.

"Talk about acting like a diva," Marcus said.

"Bryn's not like that," Zoey protested. "She's really nice. I probably should have just kept my mouth shut."

"You don't mean that, Zo," Dad said. "Setting limits with her was the right thing to do. I'm sure it's all going to turn out okay in the end."

The thing was, deep down, Zoey *had* wanted to tell Bryn what she'd told her. But right now she was upset by how things had turned out. And Dad and Marcus were the perfect targets for her frustration.

"I should never have listened to you!" she shouted, running upstairs to her room and slamming the door. She'd done all this work, upset Kate, delayed making Priti's outfit, and now it was all for nothing.

Zoey was lying on her bed feeling miserable when the doorbell rang.

"Hey, Zo," Marcus called. "Someone's here to see you."

Zoey ignored him. She wasn't in any mood for company.

A minute later there was a knock on her bedroom door.

"Zoey? It's me, Bryn. Can I come in?"

Zoey jumped up and opened the door.

Bryn stood there looking uncharacteristically shy.

"Hey, Zoey. Look . . . I'm sorry for storming off like that," she said. "It was really jerky of me. You must have thought I was being a total prima donna."

"A little," Zoey admitted.

"I don't want to be like that," Bryn said. "I really want you to be able to be honest with me, like . . . you know, a friend. I'm so sick of everyone walking on eggshells around me and pretending to like what I like and always saying yes to me because I'm famous. I was just telling one of my best friends from before I was famous how I wanted people to be real with me—and then when you *were* real with me, I freaked out."

"I guess maybe you aren't used to it anymore," Zoey said. "People being real with you, I mean."

"Yeah." Bryn sighed. "Fame has its good points, but it can also make life kind of weird sometimes. The thing is, I really like you, Zoey, and I want you to be able to be honest with me. So . . . friends?"

"Friends," Zoey said. "How about we figure out whatever last—and I mean *last*—changes you want on this outfit?"

Bryn smiled. "Sounds awesome," she said. "You're the true superstar here!"

When Priti came over that evening for a sleepover, Zoey showed her Bryn's outfit, which she had *almost* finished.

"Bryn's coming over on Tuesday night to pick it up, and then I'm going to start on yours, I promise!" Zoey said.

"I like hers because it's a Sew Zoey design, but you can see it's also got Bryn's influence," Priti said. "But I like it because when I finally get to wear *mine*, it'll be different enough from hers that no one can say I'm copying Bryn Allen."

Zoey's dad knocked on the door.

"Help! I need my fashion adviser," he said. "Is this okay for a date?"

He was wearing dark pants and a button-down shirt, with the belt Zoey had picked out for him when they had visited Daphne Shaw's studio.

"Wow! You look sharp, Mr. Webber!" exclaimed Priti.

Zoey nodded. "Priti's right, Dad. You're looking good."

"I'll see you later," Dad said. "You've got my cell phone. Marcus is here. Don't get into any mischief."

"Same for you, Dad," Zoey said.

"So who is your dad going out with?" Priti asked after Mr. Webber left.

"I don't know," Zoey confessed. "Marcus and I call her the Mystery Lady. He just met her, but he won't tell us anything about her except that she's nice."

She picked at her bedspread. "It kind of freaks me out a little, though, if you want to know the truth."

"I hate the thought of my parents dating other people," Priti said with a shudder.

"It's a little different for me because Mom's not here," Zoey said. "And I don't want Dad to be lonely. But, yeah, I worry if I'm going to like the Mystery Lady, and if she has kids, and will life change, and all that stuff. But since he says he's not ready to introduce her to me and Marcus, I guess I'm overthinking it."

"I hope my parents don't start dating for a *really* long time," Priti said. "Maybe not forever. I don't even want to *think* about it!"

When Bryn's limousine pulled up on Tuesday after school, Kate, Allie, Priti, Libby, and Marcus were all there to say hi to her. Bryn signed autographs for Libby and Priti, who hadn't yet met her.

"Allie, my friends all love the accessories you made," Bryn said. "I think you're going to be getting some orders."

Allie blushed. "That's great!" she said. "I'm just glad you like them."

When Bryn saw the finished outfit, she was thrilled.

"It's perfect!" she said, hugging Zoey. "I can't wait to wear it!"

"It was worth all the extra work in the end," Zoey said. "I think it came out really well."

"I enjoyed working with you, Zoey," Bryn said. "Let's keep in touch, okay? I'm hoping I can order some more outfits. And maybe . . . you can, you know, help me keep it real?"

"Oh, Zoey can definitely do that," Priti said. "She's great at keeping it real."

"Promise?" Bryn said, smiling at Zoey.

"You've got yourself a real deal," Zoey said, giving Bryn a hug.

CHAPTER 11

Speaking Up Is Hard to Do

Sometimes it's hard to say what's really on your mind—especially if you're afraid of losing a friendship or hurting someone else's feelings. But it's worth it in the end, even if things don't go so well at first, because it feels so much better than bottling everything up inside and getting all mad and resentful. The hard part is getting up the courage to open your mouth when you don't want to rock the boat.

Speaking of rocking the boat, that's something Kate and I are going to do at the midseason tap recital. I'm making really cool accessories for everyone in my class to pin to their outfits and to wear—sparkly things for the girls' hair and cute leather cuffs for the boys' wrists. Kate's helping me with the hair ornaments—she's taken some home to work on, so we can get them all done in time for the performance. We're determined to shine in more ways than one!

"Wait! You're back in black!" Zoey exclaimed when she saw Priti at school the following morning. "Did your parents agree?"

"Yes!" Priti said. "Mom talked to Dad and told him how I feel about everything else being decided for me. She persuaded him that maybe letting me make my own clothing choices was a battle they should let me win right now—even if in their eyes, it makes me look like an 'old widow woman' instead of a soon-to-be teenager."

Zoey laughed. "Trust me, Priti, you don't look anything like an *old widow woman*."

"I know. Especially when I wear the new outfit you're making me!"

"Well, now that I'm *finally* done with Bryn's outfit, I've started on yours. I should be able to get it done this weekend. That's if you don't make me do a zillion little alterations like Bryn!"

"Yay! I can't wait!" Priti said. "But in the meantime, I need to do something about the Miles situation. I feel bad that I've been stringing him along."

"So you've decided what you want to do?"

"Yes. Finally. But . . . can you come with me when I talk to him?" Priti asked. "I need moral support."

Zoey felt weird about being the third wheel when Priti told Miles how she felt about him. But she wanted to be a good friend.

"I guess," she said. "If you think it won't be too awkward for me to be there."

"*I'll* feel too awkward if I have to do it by

myself," Priti said. "Come on, let's go find him now, so I don't have to worry about it all morning."

They tracked down Miles by his locker.

Zoey stood nearby, but looked away, as if she weren't listening. But of course she was.

"Hey, Miles," Priti said. "Thanks for your note. And the necklace. It was really sweet of you. . . ."

She paused, clearing her throat. "It's just that . . . well, I was hoping we could just be friends. You know, instead of being more than friends."

"I kind of figured that," Miles said with a rueful smile. "Seeing as you haven't been wearing the necklace."

"It's not that I don't like you," Priti said. "I do. It's just that I met this guy Nick over the summer at camp, and we've been writing to each other, and I guess that's about all I can handle right now."

"That's okay," Miles said. "I understand."

"So . . . are you going to go back to dressing the way you did before, now that you're not trying to impress me?" Priti asked.

"I don't think I am," Miles said. "I've gotten used to seeing myself this way, and I kind of like my natural hair color now. I *definitely* get a lot less hassle from my parents."

"Tell me about it!" Priti said.

"I think maybe I was hiding behind all the black because I was shy, and I felt insecure about being the new guy at Mapleton Prep last year. Now that I'm used to being here, I don't need it anymore." He sighed. "And it's sad, but people treat me better when I'm dressed like this—they don't act like I'm some kind of freak."

Zoey realized she was guilty of thinking of Miles a certain way last year because of what he was wearing, and she felt bad. Priti was dressing the same way as Miles had been dressing, but Zoey knew that Priti was still the same person underneath.

"So what about you?" Miles asked Priti. "Are you going to go back to your old style?"

Zoey held her breath, waiting for Priti's answer. She hoped Priti would wear her special outfit at least once!

"I'm not sure," Priti replied. "It feels right for me to dress in black—for now, at least. I like looking different from the way I always have, because, well, my life is different from the way it's always been. I don't care if I get some stares. It's dramatic in a way that feels okay with me."

"Funny how we ended up with complete fashion role reversal, isn't it?" Miles said.

"I know," Priti agreed. "So . . . can we be friends?"

"Yeah," Miles said. "I think I can swing that."

Zoey could tell from his voice that he still wished it could be more. But being friends with Priti had to be more comfortable for him than being kept on a string, right?

Kate came over after school that afternoon to practice the tap routine for the midseason recital the following week. Priti joined them, because she'd taken tap herself, and she'd offered to show them some fine-tuning tricks.

"Make sure you smile big," she said. "And remember your jazz hands. It'll give you a little more wow factor."

"Or in my case, jazz hand," Kate joked. "Because I can only use one."

Zoey and Kate did the routine again, this time with

wide smiles and jazz hands—or in Kate's case, hand.

"See, I told you!" Priti said, dancing a little jig. "That was totally wowza!"

Priti was beginning to show more of her sparkly side again, even if she was still wearing dark clothes, Zoey thought. Maybe eventually she'd start showing some outward signs of sparkle again too.

The doorbell rang.

"Ooh! That must be Aunt Lulu!" Zoey said. "She's bringing Buttons over to stay!"

Buttons came romping in as soon as Zoey opened the door, giving Zoey and her friends affectionate licks.

"I can see Buttons is excited for her stay at Camp Webber," Aunt Lulu said. "But not nearly as excited as I am for our vacation in the Caribbean."

She smiled at John, who was carrying a box filled with Buttons's food, treats, and other supplies.

John grinned back at Aunt Lulu. "I'm pretty excited myself," he said.

"Well, Buttons is going to have a fantastic time with us, aren't you?" Zoey said.

Buttons wagged her tail and barked.

"I'm sorry we're going to miss your tap recital," Aunt Lulu said.

"That's okay," Zoey said. "We can give you a sneak preview!"

With Priti calling out the beat, she and Kate did a brief number for Aunt Lulu and John, who applauded wildly when they were done.

"Brava!" Aunt Lulu cheered. "We've got to head out—got an early flight tomorrow. Break a leg—except you, Kate; please don't break or strain anything else, because we want you back on the soccer field. Zo, I'll try to bring you back some cool fabric from the islands."

"And a Caribbean string instrument of some kind for Marcus," John added.

"Have fun!" Zoey said.

"Don't worry," Aunt Lulu said. "We plan to!"

Zoey worked hard over the weekend to finish Priti's outfit. She brought it to school on Monday and gave it to her friend before classes started.

"I love it!" Priti exclaimed. "It's my favorite outfit ever!"

Even Libby and Kate, who weren't that crazy about Priti's new look, confessed that they liked the design when Priti held it against herself.

"It suits you, Priti," Libby said.

"I think I'm getting used to seeing you in dark colors," Kate admitted. "It's grown on me. And Zoey's design is really fab."

"I'm so excited to wear it!" Priti said. "It was worth the wait."

On Wednesday, the night of the tap recital, Kate and Zoey gave the rest of the dancers in their class the sparkly hair ornaments, cuffs, and leotard decorations that they'd made.

"Wonderful," their tap teacher said. "They'll add pizzazz and flair to our number."

They were waiting backstage when Zoey saw Josie, the French student, standing with a group of the more advanced students.

"Hi, Josie!" she said. "I didn't know you did tap!"

"I took dance lessons in Paris," Josie said. "My mother thought it would be a good way for me to meet people."

"No wonder you're in the advanced class," Kate said. "We're just beginners."

"Well, break a leg," Zoey said.

Josie looked taken aback, and Zoey realized she might not understand that it was a theater expression.

"It's a theater phrase that means 'good luck,'" she said. "I don't really mean for you to break a leg."

"Oh, *je vois!*" Josie said, clearly relieved. "You too, then. Break your leg."

Zoey giggled. She knew what Josie meant, even though she hadn't got the expression quite right.

When Kate and Zoey's class took the stage, Zoey was ready to sparkle. She started off fine and was enjoying performing until she caught sight of Gabe in the audience—and realized he must be there to see Josie, because she hadn't told him about the recital. When she'd seen Gabe in the audience at the karaoke competition in school, he'd made her feel more relaxed, but this time—this time it threw her off her routine.

Kate glanced over at her, worried, since she missed a few steps.

Zoey took a really deep breath. *Gabe or no Gabe, the show must go on!* she told herself. She got back on step and made sure not to look in his direction again. The rest of the performance went well.

When the show was over, Priti and Libby were waiting to see Kate and Zoey. Priti was wearing the goth-inspired outfit Zoey had made for her, and she glowed, despite wearing the dark fabric.

"You guys were awesome!" Libby said. "I can't believe you just started taking tap!"

"The accessories added to the wow factor," Priti said. "Just like the cool moves I showed you."

Zoey caught sight of Josie and Gabe. They were hugging. It made her jealous, but she also realized they were kind of a cute couple.

Priti followed the line of Zoey's gaze.

"Is that why you got distracted?" she asked. "Because you saw Gabe?"

Zoey nodded.

"But, Zo, you only started liking him recently," Libby pointed out. "For all you know, it was after he started having a crush on Josie."

That was true, Zoey thought. She'd liked him as a friend before, but not *liked* liked him. "You're right," she said. "Maybe I should just try to be happy for Gabe and Josie."

"Well, you can try right now, because they're coming over here," Kate said.

"Zoey, you broke the leg very well!" Josie said.

Gabe looked confused, but Kate and Zoey laughed.

"You too, Josie," Kate said.

"How's the Etsy site going?" Gabe asked Zoey.

"Pretty well, thanks," Zoey said. "I've had more page views and questions about products since you took the new pictures. And I've had some orders from Bryn Allen's friends, but I'm not sure if that's because of the pictures or because of Bryn and her star power."

"Definitely the pictures," Gabe joked.

"Yeah, definitely." Zoey smiled. Gabe was a good friend. She was going to make a big effort to be happy for him and Josie. "Thanks again for taking them."

Zoey and Josie were waiting in the lunch line on Friday when Ivy walked into the cafeteria with Shannon and Bree.

"Can you believe what she's wearing?" Ivy said loudly, pointing at Zoey's tent dress.

Zoey ignored her, as usual.

"I still can't believe she won Best Dressed last year," Bree said.

"I know, right?" Shannon added.

Zoey couldn't believe it. Shannon was joining in with Bree and Ivy after Zoey had spent so much time helping Shannon pick out outfits.

Josie looked at Zoey and whispered, "Are they speaking about you?"

Zoey nodded.

Josie turned to face Ivy, her hands on her hips.

"I *can* believe Zoey won Best Dressed," she said. "She is very . . . how you say it? *Fashionable*. In Paris, she would fit right in."

Ivy stood with her mouth hanging open. She wasn't used to being talked back to.

"Well . . . maybe she should go live in *Paris*, then," Ivy said.

"I'd love for Zoey to visit me, anytime," Josie said. "The shopping is *formidable*."

"Thanks," Zoey told Josie afterward. "That was awesome!"

"It's nothing," Josie said. "It's what friends do, *non*?"

Zoey thought about all the times that Shannon had stood by and said nothing, or joined in when Ivy had been mean to her.

"You're right," she said. "It's what friends do."

When Shannon called Zoey on Sunday and asked if she wanted to hang out, as if nothing had happened, Zoey was taken aback.

"Don't forget, Daisy wants you to make her a special outfit," Shannon said. "She's been bugging me nonstop, asking me when you can make it for her."

Zoey thought about how she'd hesitated to speak up when Bryn kept asking her to make so many changes and how even though it was uncomfortable to have the conversation with her, it was the right thing to do. She realized it was *way* past time for her to let Shannon know how she was feeling.

"Shannon, I'm not so sure I want to hang out anymore," Zoey said, "because it seems like you only want to be my friend when you need something— like fashion advice or for me to make an outfit for Daisy, so she'll stop bugging you."

"I—"

"I don't want to be your secret stylist," Zoey continued. "And it hurts when you just stand there when Ivy says mean things about me, or worse, when you join in. So if you can't be up front with Ivy and Bree about the fact that we're friends, then I don't want to hang out anymore."

Shannon was quiet, and then she said, "I'm sorry, Zoey. I didn't mean to hurt your feelings. I just didn't think about how it would look to you, I guess."

Zoey wondered how Shannon thought it *would* look to her. How could she have imagined it would feel anything but bad to have Ivy saying such nasty things?

"I have to think about it," Shannon continued.

"I want us to be friends again, but I'm just not sure I'm ready to go public yet."

Hearing that was a big disappointment, but it made Zoey all the more glad that she'd finally spoken up about how she felt.

"Okay," she said. "Well, the door is always open if you change your mind. And tell Daisy I will make her an outfit when I have the time."

"Thanks, Zoey," Shannon said. "And . . . I'm sorry."

"Whoa, Zo," Marcus exclaimed when Zoey came into the kitchen after her conversation with Shannon. "You need to turn that frown upside down."

"I can't," Zoey said. "It doesn't feel so great when you find out that you've been wrong about a friend."

"Let me guess," Marcus said. "Shannon?"

"Yeah." Zoey sighed.

"Things might still change," Marcus said. "But in the meantime, you've got some great other friends, right?"

"The best," Zoey said. "*They* aren't ashamed of me."

Just then Allie burst through the back door, waving a magazine.

"Zoey! Look!" she said, putting a copy of *Celebrity* magazine on the table in front of Zoey and Marcus.

Right on the cover was a picture of Bryn Allen—wearing Zoey's outfit!

"Oh my gosh!" Zoey exclaimed. "My outfit is on the cover!"

Buttons scampered around her feet, barking excitedly.

"What was that about someone being ashamed of you?" Marcus grinned. "Anyone in their right mind would be proud to be friends with up-and-coming designer Zoey Webber."

"I know *I* am!" Allie said.

Zoey looked at the magazine cover and clutched it to her chest. Shannon might be ashamed of being friends with her, but she was feeling pretty proud of herself!

CHAPTER 12

Celebritation!

I almost fell off my chair when Allie came over with *Celebrity* magazine yesterday, and there was a picture of Bryn Allen wearing the outfit I made her ON THE COVER!!!! Can you imagine? Dad says he's going to frame it for me, so I can hang it over my worktable, next to Marie Antoinette.

It was just as great to see Priti wearing the original design that inspired Bryn's outfit at my tap recital. It looked great on her, and, well, it made me realize that she doesn't need all the glitzy accessories because Priti has an inner sparkle all her own. That's what makes her Priti!

It's strange—just when I think things couldn't possibly get any more exciting, something even more awesome happens when I least expect it. That's what inspired today's design. It's like Sew Zoey has helped me to climb to ever-higher peaks. If only I could peek into the future to see what happens next!

A few days later, Zoey was called down to Ms. Austen's office.

"Congratulations," Ms. Austen said. "I hear one of your outfits made the cover of *Celebrity* magazine. *Very* exciting!"

Zoey couldn't quite picture Ms. Austen reading *Celebrity* magazine.

"I know!" she said. "I'm already getting a lot

more hits on my blog and my Etsy store."

"You deserve it, Zoey," Ms. Austen said. "You've been working very hard." She pulled a small padded envelope out of her desk drawer. "It looks like someone else has been noticing your hard work too. You've got a present from Daphne Shaw. Her assistant called yesterday and said they were mailing something to school overnight. They didn't want to send it to your house in case no one was home to sign for it."

Zoey hadn't told many people that Fashionista was Daphne Shaw, but Daphne had told Zoey to loop in Ms. Austen. Zoey opened the little parcel, and inside was a necklace with a pendant made of a miniature copy of the *Celebrity* magazine cover. The card attached said:

Congratulations on reaching
another milestone—your
first celebrity cover shot!
Onward and upward!

—Daphne Shaw

"I can't believe she knew about it and had this made up already!" Zoey exclaimed.

"It looks like your fashion fairy godmother keeps close tabs on you," Ms. Austen said. "You're lucky to have such a wonderful mentor."

"I know," Zoey said, genuinely grateful as she put on the necklace. "I'm lucky in lots and *lots* of ways."

A few days later, Aunt Lulu and John were back from their Caribbean getaway. They came over for dinner that night to share stories about their trip and to pick up Buttons from "camp."

"We got you a cuatro," John said, handing it to Marcus. "The band at the hotel recommended this one."

"Cool!" Marcus said, strumming it to test the tuning. "Thanks!"

"Make lots of great music," Aunt Lulu told him. "And this is for you, Zoey."

She handed Zoey a package. Inside was Caribbean coral reef batik fabric in beautiful shades of dark blue and turquoise.

"Ooh! I love it!" Zoey said.

"I can't wait to see what you make from it," John said. "You're so creative."

"She is," Aunt Lulu agreed. "Just like her mom."

Zoey wished she had more memories of her mother. Aunt Lulu was the closet thing she had to a mom, being her mother's sister. She and Dad were great, telling her stories about her mother and how she was so creative, making her own clothes and experimenting with designs. But it wasn't the same as having a mother to talk to and share things with every day.

"Oh! I almost forgot!" Aunt Lulu said, reaching into her bag and bringing out a copy of the *Celebrity* magazine with Bryn Allen wearing Zoey's outfit on the cover. "I was relaxing on the plane, reading *Celebrity* magazine, when all of a sudden I saw that the outfit Bryn Allen was wearing on the cover was made 'by her friend Zoey Webber of Sew Zoey!'"

"She practically jumped out of her seat," John said. "I almost got a lap full of hot coffee!"

"Well, it's not every day I see my niece's design

being worn by a TV star on the cover of *Celebrity* magazine," Aunt Lulu said. "I was excited. Can you blame me?"

"Of course not, honey," John said, gazing at Aunt Lulu fondly. "I was pretty excited myself."

"You should have seen Allie when she brought it over," Marcus said. "She was flipping out too."

"It was a red-letter day for all of us," Dad said.

Zoey showed her aunt and John the necklace Daphne Shaw sent to commemorate her first celebrity cover shot.

"You really are going onward and upward, Zo," Aunt Lulu said. "I'm so proud of you."

"That makes two of us," John said.

Aunt Lulu and John exchanged meaningful looks.

"Speaking of the two of us," Aunt Lulu said. "We have some big news to announce."

"What's that?" Zoey asked.

"While we were on vacation, John asked me to marry him," Aunt Lulu said, a radiant smile lighting up her face.

"And your answer was?" Marcus asked.

"Fortunately for me, her answer was yes," John said.

"*Oh my gosh!* You're getting married?!" Zoey exclaimed.

"Looks like it," Aunt Lulu said. "We're going shopping for a ring this weekend."

"And she already promised me she would," John said. "No backing out now, Lulu!"

"I've already bought a cake to celebrate," Dad said, going to the fridge and taking out a cake that had "Congrats, Lulu & John!" written on it.

"Wait . . . but how did you know, Dad?" Zoey asked.

"Oh, a little bird texted me to give me the good news, but asked me to keep it a secret until she could tell you herself," Dad said with a smile.

Dad opened a bottle of champagne for the grown-ups and poured sparkling apple cider into champagne flutes for Marcus and Zoey.

"A toast," he said. "To John and Lulu—may the love you share now endure and grow."

They all clinked glasses and sipped.

"I'd like to propose a toast too," John said. "To

the wonderful Webbers—for welcoming me into the family."

"It wasn't hard," Marcus said. "You're a pretty cool guy."

"Yeah," Zoey agreed. "You fit in easily."

"Well, I'm looking forward making this whole uncle thing official," John said. "I hope you feel okay about it too."

Zoey felt a little weird about it, if she had to be honest. It was going to take some getting used to, calling him Uncle John. But she'd grown to love John almost as much as she loved Aunt Lulu, and it was great to see her aunt so happy.

Buttons put her paws on John's knee. He lifted her onto his lap, and she licked his face. Buttons seemed perfectly happy with the situation.

"I'm more than okay with it," Zoey said.

Okay, so the fabric of Zoey's family was changing. But that wasn't necessarily a bad thing—just like updating a design to make it fresh, life sometimes needed a change of lace too.

Sew excited to keep
reading?
Turn the page for a
sneak peek at the next book
in the *Sew Zoey* series:

BURSTING
AT THE
seams

Runway Ready!

Hello, readers!! So, remember when the dress I designed for Bryn Allen was on the cover of *Celebrity* magazine? I do! In fact, it's hard to forget. Since then, I've been getting some e-mails and requests through my Sew Zoey store for more fashion forward looks. I'm not sure that's my speed, exactly, but here's a design that could look great on someone young, without showing too much. The problem is that making it would probably take me thirty or forty hours, which is a *lot* for one dress! I'd need a nice, long vacation afterward. ☺

And speaking of vacations . . . my most favorite aunt, Lulu, is finally back in town after a romantic Caribbean getaway with her (dum dee dum) new fiancé! She and John got engaged while they were on their trip. I'm meeting her for tea and cupcakes after school to get all the juicy details. I'm SEW pumped to see her!

Zoey Webber was in heaven. She was at her favorite café, Tea Time, with a cup of oolong tea, a pink frosted cupcake, and her aunt Lulu. Lulu was tanned and smiling as she drizzled honey into her English breakfast tea and stirred it with a spoon.

"Tell me *everything*," Zoey said. "Don't leave anything out! I want to feel like I was there too!"

Lulu laughed, and began to unwrap the bag that held her croissant. "Well, it *was* pretty magical. Everything about Barbados is magical, really. John and I were out to dinner, at a beautiful restaurant built on a cliff at the edge of the ocean. We were watching tiny nurse sharks swim up for chum the restaurant throws them, and when I looked away from the sharks, John was kneeling beside me."

"And?" urged Zoey. She was so enthralled with the story, she hadn't even touched her tea or her cupcake yet. "Did you say yes immediately, or did you cry, or what?"

Lulu laughed again. "Let's just say my eyes were teary, but I was so happy. And I said yes right away. I think I *might* have even shouted it. The people sitting at tables around us applauded, and that was it."

"Sounds *perfect*." Zoey sighed with satisfaction. The story was exactly what she would have wished for her aunt, who had always been more of a second mother to Zoey since her own mom had passed away when she was very little. Although it had been somewhat hard for Zoey when Lulu and John had first begun dating, because she'd been worried she'd lose *her* special place in Lulu's life, that hadn't happened at all. Zoey felt sure that adding John Chadden to their family would make things even better.

With the proposal story out of the way, Zoey bit into her cupcake with enthusiasm. It was Friday afternoon, and a long and busy week at school had made her ravenous. She was so focused on her cupcake, in fact, that she didn't notice Lulu wasn't touching her own croissant.

When Zoey finally looked up, Lulu was leaning forward in her seat, her eyes bright and her lips clamped together. A smile tugged at the corners of her mouth.

"What is it?" Zoey asked. "Why are you looking at me like that?" Self-conscious, Zoey wiped at her mouth with a napkin, in case she was covered in extra frosting.

"There's a *tiny* bit more to the story . . . ," Lulu

said. She giggled and then clapped a hand over her mouth to stop. "But before I tell you, you have to *swear* to keep it a secret."

Zoey felt her heart begin to pound. More to the story? Like what? Her aunt was acting very strangely, and not at all like the calm, cool, interior designer and business owner that she was.

"Tell me!" Zoey exclaimed.

Lulu placed her hands on either side of the café table, as if to anchor herself so she wouldn't fall over, and whispered, "John and I are having a surprise wedding, and it's in three weeks!"

Zoey stared at her aunt, her mouth hanging open. A *surprise* wedding? What on Earth was that? In three *weeks*?

Zoey shook her head, unable to spit out a sentence. All she could mumble was *"What?"*

Aunt Lulu giggled again, her sparkling eyes and flushed cheeks making her look every bit the happy and excited bride-to-be. "We've decided to invite our close friends and family to a little 'engagement party' at my house in a few weeks. At least, that's what they'll think. But when everyone arrives, we're really going to surprise them and tell them we'll be getting married that night!"

Zoey had never heard of a surprise wedding. "So the wedding, the *actual* wedding where you say your vows, is in *three weeks* at your house, but no one will know except you and John and me?"

Lulu nodded. "And a few other close family members, like your dad and brother. And the vendors. We'll have a caterer and a cake and flowers and a photographer, like a normal wedding. But it'll all just be a little more casual and fun, since it'll be at my house and no one will expect it."

Zoey's mind reeled with the possibilities. No church, no big reception hall. No waiting months and months for the big day. A surprise wedding for her aunt, in just three weeks. And she was one of the few in on the secret!

"I LOVE IT!" Zoey screeched, and several people in the café turned to glance at her. Lulu and Zoey looked at each other and grinned. "I really do, Aunt Lulu. This is so *you*."

Lulu winked at her. "Exactly. John and I have both been married before, and we didn't want to do the big wedding thing again. We love each other, and we want to start our life together *now*. And the surprise just makes it so much more fun!" She paused, taking a sip of her tea and then carefully placing the teacup back on its saucer. "And there's something very special I'd like to ask you, Zoey."

"I'm not sure I can take any more exciting news, Aunt Lulu," Zoey said honestly. "I'm already on a sugar high from the cupcake, and now I know the biggest secret ever!"

Aunt Lulu put her hand over Zoey's and squeezed it. "I'd like you to be my junior bridesmaid, honey. And I'd really love it if you'd come shopping with me and help me pick out my dress."

Zoey was honored. Truly honored. She'd get to stand up with her aunt at the wedding *and* help find the dress. It was a dream come true!

"Of course, yes to both!" Zoey said. "I can't wait!"

"My maid of honor will be my best friend, Sybil, but since she lives in Atlanta, she won't be here to shop with me. I'd like for you and her to wear dresses that coordinate, at least in color. She'll buy hers, but I think it would be wonderful if you designed and made your own junior bridesmaid's dress."

Design her own junior bridesmaid's dress? Zoey was flabbergasted. With that final piece of exciting news, Zoey jumped up from her seat and threw her arms around her aunt. What could be more fun? She'd make the most beautiful junior bridesmaid's dress in the world!

Aunt Lulu hugged Zoey back, smoothing Zoey's hair with one hand. "I take it that's a yes?"

Zoey nodded and gave her aunt one more big squeeze before returning to her seat. A really good afternoon for Zoey was a cupcake and conversation with her aunt. Hearing about a marriage proposal made it extra special. Finding out about a secret wedding made it unbelievable. Hearing that she'd be a junior bridesmaid *and* get to design her own dress? Zoey didn't have a word for it.

"I think I might burst," she told Lulu. "I think I'm going to burst right through the walls of Tea Time."

Lulu chuckled. "Well, if possible, *don't*. And remember, the only people you can discuss this with are Marcus and your father. We have to keep it a secret so that the surprise works. It's very important to John and me. Promise?"

Zoey nodded. "I promise," she said.

She had no idea how difficult that promise would be to keep. . . .

The next morning, Lulu picked up Zoey, and they drove to a fancy bridal salon. Zoey had never been wedding dress shopping before, and she couldn't even remember the last wedding she'd attended. Probably her cousin's wedding when Zoey was about seven. She had no idea what to expect when they walked in.

A chic, middle-aged woman in a fitted black suit approached them. "Good morning. Do you have an appointment?" she asked.

"Yes, I'm Lulu Price," Aunt Lulu said.

The woman checked a clipboard, nodded, and ushered them back to a large round room, with racks and racks of gorgeous dresses on display, and a wall of dressing rooms on one side.

The consultant, Deirdre, gave Lulu a quick tour of the gowns, showing her how they were grouped by price. "And when is your wedding?" Deirdre asked, making notes on her clipboard.

With slightly pink cheeks, Lulu explained she was having a surprise wedding at her house in just three weeks, and she wanted something not too formal, but elegant, and that it needed to be ready to purchase and alter immediately.

"Three weeks?" Deirdre repeated. "*Three weeks?*"

Zoey's eyes swiveled from Lulu to Deirdre and back to Lulu. What was the big deal about three weeks?

Lulu simply nodded, and said firmly, "Yes, three weeks. What do you have that's ready to wear?"

Deirdre wrinkled her brow a moment, and looked worried, but then her face seemed to relax. "I love a challenge," she told Lulu. "Go into the dressing room, please, and I'll bring you some sample dresses available for purchase, and also a few of our consignment dresses. They can all go home with you immediately."

Lulu sighed with relief, and she and Zoey headed to the dressing room.

Zoey whispered to her aunt, "I didn't realize you

couldn't buy a wedding dress off the rack," she said. "What's the big deal?"

Lulu explained. "Most wedding dresses are made to order. So you go to a bridal store, try on a sample, and then they order it in your size. When it comes in, which can take months, you usually have to alter it some. That's what happened with my first wedding. But we don't have time for that now, so I'll just have to take what I can get."

Zoey sat, slightly worried. She wanted her aunt to have the perfect dress. She didn't want her to have to settle for whatever samples or consignment dresses were available that very second.

Deirdre knocked and came into the dressing room, her arms full of gowns.

Aunt Lulu began trying them on. Luckily, she wore a standard dress size, and was able to fit into most of the samples. The first dress, a strapless silk chiffon with seed pearls and sequins, was too formal for a fall wedding in someone's backyard. The second, a voluminous ball gown, had a skirt so wide, it would never fit through the front door of Lulu's house. The third was a possibility, with wide straps, a square décolletage, and a smooth flowy skirt. It wasn't too formal, and it looked appropriate for a surprise wedding at home. But, unfortunately, Lulu was a bit on the tall side, and the dress was three inches too short, even without heels, and the hem wasn't quite long enough to let down.

"There's no fixing a too-short dress," Lulu said with a groan. "Too long would have been a better problem."

"You could cut it and make it knee-length?" Zoey suggested. She was starting to feel discouraged by Lulu's limited options.

"I really want a long dress," Lulu said. "In fact, I really like the *top* of this dress, but with the *bottom* of that first one. It's too bad it's not like magnetic dress-up dolls where you can mix and match!"

Lulu tried on several more dresses, but none of them were right either. Everything was either too formal or fit poorly. Finally, she looked at Zoey, and blinked. "I think we've struck out," she said dejectedly.

"What if," Zoey began, an idea forming in her mind, "what if I were to sketch the top of the dress you liked, with the bottom of that other one, and you gave the sketch to a wedding seamstress and they made it for you? Could that work?"

"It's a terrific idea, Zoey," said Lulu. "But I'm afraid I tried that first! I called my regular seamstress as soon as we got back from Barbados, but she was booked solid. She even gave me some other people to try, but none of them had availability to make a dress so fast. That's why I thought I'd make do with a sample dress."

Deirdre knocked on the dressing room door, and Lulu opened it. "I'm afraid that's all we have available in your size that could be ready in time," Deirdre said. "I'm so terribly sorry! I can call you if we get any new consignment gowns in this week or next."

"Thank you," Lulu said. "Something will work out, I'm sure. I can always look online."

Deirdre removed the dresses, and Lulu put her regular clothes back on. She and Zoey left the store, packed with beautiful wedding gowns that wouldn't be ready in time for Lulu's big day.

"What are you going to do?" Zoey asked.

Lulu stopped walking and turned to Zoey. "Zoey," she said, "I know this is a lot to ask, especially with you being so busy with school, but is there any way you'd have time to make a dress for me? We could keep the design really simple, but it's the only way I can get what I want in time for the wedding! And it would mean so much to me to wear an original Sew Zoey dress on my wedding day."

Zoey couldn't believe her ears. Her aunt wanted her to make her *wedding* dress? The most important dress of her life?

"But, Aunt Lulu, I don't know *anything* about wedding dresses! I didn't even know you had to order them! I wouldn't know where to start."

"We'll design it together. Just think of it as a simple white dress. And you know a lot more than you think you do, my talented niece. Wasn't an outfit you made just on the cover of *Celebrity* magazine?"

"Well, yes." Zoey blushed. She was so honored that her aunt would even ask. "I'd *love* to, Aunt Lulu. I'd really, really love to!"

Lulu hugged her and said, "This will be great,

Zoey. Really special. It fits our surprise wedding theme, don't you think?"

Zoey agreed. It was sort of perfect.

"Why don't you think about the dresses we liked today and come up with a sketch or two? Something that won't be too hard for you to make so fast. And one more thing: I'll need the skirt fabric to be stretchy if it's fitted, because John and I plan to surprise everyone with a tango for our first dance, since we met in ballroom dance class."

"Okay!" agreed Zoey. "I already have some ideas from what we saw. And I began sketching some designs for my junior bridesmaid's dress last night. Maybe you should take me home now so I can get to work. . . ."

Lulu nodded. "Sure thing. Do you still want to come with me tomorrow for a cupcake tasting, flowers, and stationery?"

"Yes, yes, and yes!" said Zoey. "I don't want to miss *anything*!"

Lulu and Zoey linked arms and then headed for the car. They had a lot of work to do.

Great stories are like great accessories: You can never have too many! Collect all the books in the Sew Zoey series:

Ready to Wear

On Pins and Needles

Lights, Camera, Fashion!

Stitches and Stones

Cute as a Button

A Tangled Thread

Knot Too Shabby!

Swatch Out!

A Change of Lace

If you like sew Zoey books, then you'll love

CUPCAKE DIARIES!

Available at your favorite store.

CUPCAKE DIARIES
Katie and the cupcake cure
by coco simon

CUPCAKE DIARIES
Mia in the mix
by coco simon

CUPCAKE DIARIES
Emma on thin icing
by coco simon

CUPCAKE DIARIES
Alexis and the perfect recipe
by coco simon

Katie   Mia   Emma   Alexis